Cruise Control

Cruise Ship Cozy Mystery Series

Book 6

Hope Callaghan

hopecallaghan.com

Visit my website for new releases and special offers:

hopecallaghan.com

Thank you, Peggy Hyndman, Jean Pilch and Cindi Graham for taking the time to preview *Cruise Control,* for the extra sets of eyes and for catching all my mistakes.

i

D1715075

Meet the Author

Hope Callaghan is an author who loves to write Christian books, especially Christian Mystery and Cozy Mystery books. She has written more than 30 mystery books (and counting) in four series.

Born and raised in a small town in West Michigan, she now lives in Florida with her husband.

She is the proud mother of one daughter and a stepdaughter and stepson. When she's not doing the thing she loves best - writing books - she enjoys cooking, traveling and reading books.

Hope loves to connect with her readers! Connect with her today!

Visit **hopecallaghan.com** for special offers, free books, and soon-to-be-released books!

Email: hope@hopecallaghan.com

Facebook:
https://www.facebook.com/hopecallaghanauthor/

Foreword

Dear Reader,

I would like to personally thank you for purchasing this book and also to let you know that a portion of all my book sales go to support missions which proclaim the Good News of Jesus Christ.

My prayer is that you will be blessed by reading my stories and knowing that you are helping to spread the Gospel of the Lord.

With more than thirty mystery books (and counting) in four series published, I hope you will have as much fun reading them as I have writing them!

May God Bless You!

Sincerely,

Author Hope Callaghan

Table Of Contents

Chapter One

Millie Sanders, Assistant Cruise Director aboard the mega cruise ship, Siren of the Seas, glanced at her watch. "Forty-five minutes and counting."

Andy Walker, Siren of the Seas Cruise Director and Millie's boss, wrinkled his brow and crossed his arms. "I don't know what you're so nervous about, Millie. You should be thrilled that your cousins and their friends are joining us for the next seven days."

Andy was right. Millie *should* be happy she would get to spend time with her cousins, Gloria Rutherford-Kennedy and Liz Applegate. She was excited...and nervous. Her cousin, super sleuth, Gloria, had a penchant for getting into some real humdinger situations. Millie just hoped the next week would be calm and uneventful.

"I'm thrilled to see family, although Gloria seems to have a cloud of criminal activity that follows her wherever she goes."

"Hmm," Andy chuckled. "That trait obviously runs in the family."

It was true. It seemed that since Millie had joined the crew of Siren of the Seas, it had been one calamity after another, the most recent being a family that had gone missing on the remote island of Kiriban. "I can't help it if this ship has had a run of bad luck with crazed killers and sketchy crew," she argued.

"I'll be right back." Millie left Andy standing near the gangway and made her way over to the guest services desk to chat with Nikki, one of the younger crew who was also Millie's friend. "Did you happen to see if Captain Armati made it back onboard yet?"

Nikki had a bird's-eye view of all crew who had boarded since the ship docked a few hours earlier in their home port of Miami. She would be one of the first to know if the captain had returned from his extended leave. Millie was anxious to see him and his sidekick, Scout, a teacup Yorkie.

He had been gone longer than originally planned; Millie feared that perhaps he wouldn't return to Siren of the Seas, although he had assured her he had signed another contract and would be back.

"Yep. Scout and he stopped by here first thing this morning to say hi. He and Purser Donovan Sweeney went into his office and closed the door. I'm not sure what that was all about." Nikki glanced behind her and then leaned forward. "He had a serious look on his face when he came out. So did Donovan."

Millie tapped her fingernails on the countertop. Donovan was in charge of all monetary exchanges on board the ship. Not only that, but he handled crew pay and tips, and was the final say in new hires. "Maybe they fired Danielle Kneldon," she joked.

Danielle was Millie's roommate and at times, a royal pain in the rear. She was young and full of energy, and always managing to land smack dab in sticky situations, all self-inflicted, of course.

Last week Andy had put Danielle in charge of "Teen Scene," the new name he had picked out for the fourteen-to-eighteen-year-old passengers' group, and instructed her to "spice it up" with new activities to keep the teenagers entertained.

Danielle had come up with, in her words, a "brilliant" idea that morphed into a mob of fifty or so kids who descended on the "Adults Only" pool area carrying garbage bags filled with water balloons where they proceeded to terrorize the adults in the area.

Danielle claimed ignorance and said she hadn't realized it was an adults-only area, although big bold signs were plastered to the front of the doors leading into the area stating no one under the age of twenty-one was allowed.

Andy gave Danielle a stern lecture and every affected – aka wet - adult passenger received a twenty-five dollar onboard credit, which cost the cruise ship nearly a thousand dollars in comps.

Nikki shook her head. "Nope. Danielle stopped by a short time ago and said she was on break and heading back to the cabin."

Millie thanked Nikki for the information. She made her way across the lounge area and resumed her position next to Andy. They were now only minutes away from allowing the first wave of passengers, the priority passengers, to board.

Since Gloria, Liz and their friends had booked suites, they would be among the first wave of passengers allowed to board.

"Here they come," Andy announced.

Millie studied the faces as Andy and she smiled and greeted the boarding passengers. She answered several questions and the passengers' number one question was to ask where lunch was being served. She passed out several ship maps and even greeted a few of the "regulars" by name.

A familiar smile slowly emerged from the sea of faces. It was Millie's cousin, Gloria. Right behind Gloria was her other cousin, Liz, and behind the two of them were several other women.

They made their way over and gathered around. "Millie! Oh my gosh! Look at you." Gloria Kennedy hugged her cousin and quickly released her grip. "You look wonderful."

Millie smoothed the front of her jacket. The salty ocean air and warm tropical climate had been good to Millie. She'd lost a few pounds, now sported a nice golden tan and was more relaxed and at ease than she'd been in years. "Thanks. You look wonderful, too. Married life agrees with you."

Gloria had always been an attractive woman but now she positively glowed. "Thanks."

Millie turned her attention to her other cousin, Liz. Liz was the older sibling, affectionately known as the drama queen. "Liz. You look fabulous too. I love your haircut."

Liz patted her hair. "Thanks Millie."

Millie touched Andy's arm. "This is my boss and the man in charge of all the fun, Andy Walker, Cruise Director."

Gloria and Liz shook Andy's hand. "It's nice to meet you. Hopefully, we can stay out of trouble this week."

Gloria turned to the women hovering behind her. "These are our friends. Lucy, Margaret, Dot, Andrea, Ruth and Frances."

One by one, the girls shook hands with Millie and Andy. Millie vaguely recalled meeting one or two of them eons ago. "Some of your faces are familiar but it has been so long," she confessed.

"Why don't you show the girls to their suites?" Andy suggested. "I can hold down the fort for a few minutes."

Millie nodded. "If you don't mind. I'll be right back." She turned to the women. "What are your suite numbers?"

Gloria unfolded the piece of paper she was holding in her hand. "We're in suite 11212 and the others are right next door or across the hall...I think."

"Follow me." Millie led them to the bank of glass elevators and pushed the *up* button on the wall beside them. "Take this elevator to deck eleven and I'll meet you there." She left them by the elevator and headed to the stairs.

Millie was waiting for them when the elevator doors opened and they followed her down a long hall toward the front of the ship. They stopped in front of a door with the numbers 11212 etched on the front of a tropical turquoise plaque.

"This is it," Millie announced. "What are the other numbers?" The girls recited the numbers. Margaret, Dot and Ruth were in the suite next door to Gloria, Andrea and Lucy. Frances and Liz were directly across the hall.

Frances and Liz headed to their suite across the hall while Margaret opened the door to their suite and Margaret, along with Dot and Ruth, disappeared inside.

Gloria inserted her key card. The door beeped. She grasped the handle and pushed the door open.

"Wow!" She stepped inside and slowly inspected the spacious suite. Near the entrance door and to the right were a set of doors. She opened one of the doors and peeked in. "What a roomy closet," she reported.

Andrea eased around Gloria and opened the door on the left. "The bathroom." She opened the door wider and stepped inside. "Not too shabby."

Millie followed the trio inside. She had never been inside one of the suites; there had never been a need and she was curious to see what the luxurious cabins looked like.

The bathroom was large, almost as large as Millie and Danielle's entire shared cabin. On one wall was a large jetted tub. On the other wall, and in a separate room was the toilet. Two double sinks separated the tub from the toilet. "I'm gonna come stay with you guys this week," Millie joked.

The women made their way into the main cabin. Off to one side were double beds and across from the beds a long vanity and large mirror. Beyond the beds was another room.

Inside the room was a sitting area, complete with full size couch, coffee table and side chair. On the opposite wall was a flat screen television.

Two sets of sliding glass doors led to a balcony.

"Let's check out the balcony," Lucy said excitedly.

The girls stepped out onto the balcony, which faced the cruise ship terminal.

"Hello over there." Dot's head peeked around the corner of a partition on the far side of their balcony.

"Watch this." Millie stepped over to the frosted glass door. She pulled a set of keys from her front pocket, inserted the key in a small slot off to one side, and the connecting door swung open. "You can leave this open if you want."

Millie looked around and quickly realized the suites were located in the front of the ship. She shaded her eyes and gazed down at the corner of the bridge. "That's the ship's bridge," she told the girls. "Look. You can catch a glimpse of the interior through the corner of the windows."

Liz, who had finished her own suite inspection, wandered out onto the balcony and peered over Millie's shoulder. "That's the outboard bridge wing," she informed them. "There's a glass pane in the floor for the captain and crew to visually navigate the ship when docking or leaving port."

Millie had never noticed a glass pane in the bridge floor. "Well, I'll be darned. I had no idea. I'll have to check it out next time I'm in the bridge, maybe when I give you a tour."

She glanced at her watch. "I better get back to work," she said. "Lunch is being served out on the lido deck and also in Waves, the buffet area. Both are on this floor and located in the back of the ship."

She left the girls on the balcony and headed back down to deck five. A large group of guests crowded around Andy. Millie hurried over to help her boss, answering questions and directing passengers.

Two men, who were wearing black suits and had serious expressions on their faces, passed by.

Millie watched as they stepped over to the guest services desk.

She had never seen the men before and wondered what they were doing. They definitely weren't passengers. "I wonder what that's all about."

Millie nodded her head in that direction and Andy followed her gaze. "I have no idea," he said.

She remembered Nikki mentioning Captain Armati had gone into Donovan Sweeney's office. When they emerged, they wore serious expressions on their faces, not unlike these men.

Nikki strode out from behind the desk and led the men in the dark suits through the atrium and out of sight. Millie could've sworn she caught a glimpse of a gun hidden under one of the men's jackets. "I think I saw a gun," she whispered to Andy. He didn't have time to reply as a fresh wave of passengers descended on them.

It was another two hours before the crew finally closed the door and removed the massive glass and brass passenger ramp.

"Whew! I'm starving." Millie swiped a stray strand of hair from her eyes and tucked it behind her ear. "I think I'll grab a bite to eat."

Andy nodded. "I'll meet you in Waves in a few minutes. I want to stop by the bridge to welcome Captain Armati back first."

Millie would have loved to do the same, but it wasn't her place. She would have time later, after the ship set sail. She was sure the captain had his hands full trying to get up to speed, not to mention navigate the ship out of port and into open water.

"Sounds like a plan." Millie watched Andy head to the bank of elevators while she made her way over to talk to Nikki. Luckily, no passengers were at the guest services desk. Nikki looked up when Millie got close.

She didn't bother beating around the bush. "So what was up with the suits?" Millie asked.

Nikki closed the black book in front of her, folded her hands and set them on top. "One of them flashed a badge and said his name was Johnson and Captain Armati was expecting him so I called up to the bridge and the captain told me to bring them up."

She frowned. "It was odd. When we got there, the captain took them into the bridge and then asked me to wait outside, that they wouldn't be long. So I hung around and not twenty minutes later, the men emerged and I escorted them to the exit."

"The men left the ship?" Millie asked.

"Yep." Nikki nodded. "They weren't much for conversation. I tried to talk to one of them but he looked at me like I was stupid so I shut up."

Millie thanked Nikki for the information and headed to the buffet area. The kitchen crew had switched up the menu and today's lunch theme was "A Taste of Tuscany," which included a tempting variety of Italian dishes.

Millie, who had missed breakfast, loaded her plate with lasagna, pepperoni pizza and parmesan chicken. She even managed to make room for a couple garlic bread knots.

She headed to a corner table where she eased into a seat facing the buffet so she could keep an eye out for Andy. Millie tried to eat in the same spot to make it easier for Andy and her friends to find her if they happened to share the same breaks.

Millie spied the top of Andy's bright red hair and then caught his eye. She wondered if Captain Armati had told him who the mysterious men in the suits were.

Andy set his tray of food on the table, pulled out the chair opposite Millie and plopped down. He placed his napkin in his lap and leaned his elbows on the table. "The ship is on extra security alert," he said.

Chapter Two

Millie set her fork on her plate, her full attention on Andy. "What makes you say that?" She had a sneaky suspicion it had something to do with the men in the dark suits.

"Because Captain Armati told me they were bringing a few extra security guards onboard to cover more of the passenger areas."

"How many extra security guards?"

Andy shrugged. "He didn't say. Said Donovan Sweeney had all the pertinent information but not to mention it to the other staff or crew. He said no one should even notice."

Millie tore a chunk of her crusty bread and dipped it in the lasagna sauce. She had never known the ship to bring on extra security guards, especially on short notice. Every person employed by the cruise line went through a rigorous background check and it took weeks, sometimes months, to complete the process.

Obviously, someone even higher up than Captain Armati had authorized the extra security. Millie knew many, but not all of the employees onboard Siren of the Seas.

"The only thing he told me is they would be scattered about the ship working in various areas."

"Including entertainment?"

"Yep." He nodded.

It would be nearly impossible to figure out who the extra employees would be. Every week there were new crewmembers joining the ship, along with those returning from break or transferring from a sister ship to begin working on Siren of the Seas.

Andy finished his last bite of chicken, wiped his mouth with his napkin and set the napkin, along with his fork, on top of the empty plate. "Why don't you give your family a tour of the ship after making your rounds? I won't need you backstage until later, before the first headliner show, Gem of the Seas, begins."

"That would be wonderful," Millie smiled. "I'm heading up to lido to check in with Zack and the sail away party before making a run by the youth area to check on Danielle."

"Good idea. Hard telling what brilliant new idea Danielle has come up with this week for our young passengers." Andy slid his chair back and stood as he reached for his tray of dirty dishes.

Millie watched Andy zigzag around the dining tables, nodding to guests and stopping to chat with a couple of them before he disappeared through the sliding glass doors.

She quickly finished her food and carried her tray to the bin near the door. The lido deck and pool area were on the other side of the buffet area.

Strains of music from the steel drums wafted through the air. Millie loved the tropical island tunes and even after all of these months of working onboard the ship, she hadn't grown tired of hearing them.

The party was in full swing with Zack leading the passengers in a rousing rendition of the Macarena.

Millie caught a glimpse of Gloria and Liz, right in the thick of the action and she grinned. She could see the other girls, Gloria and Liz's friends, dancing as well.

Millie caught Gloria's eye and her cousin slipped out of the crowd and made her way over.

"Looks like fun." Millie said. "Zack is one of my favorite dancers. He's a hoot!"

A breathless, bright-eyed Gloria nodded. "Yeah. I can't believe how much fun we're having," she gushed.

"I have to make my rounds right now, but Andy suggested I give you and the girls a tour of the ship, if you're interested," Millie said.

Gloria wiped the perspiration from her brow and nodded. "Sounds great. What time?"

"Give me an hour and I'll meet you over there." Millie pointed to the tiki bar in the corner of the lido deck, right next to the towel station.

"Gotcha."

Millie watched as Gloria rejoined her friends before making her way to the railing. She paused to pick up a dirty plate and empty cocktail glass before heading down the side steps.

Her first stop was "The Shed," the activity center for the nine to eleven year old passengers. One of the other crew, a young man Millie had seen before but for the life of her couldn't remember his name, was talking to a group of passengers. Millie gave a small wave and continued her rounds.

The Teen Scene, the group Danielle was in charge of, was next door and she could hear hip-hop music blaring through the closed door. Millie opened the door and peeked inside.

Danielle and a large group of teens had gathered in a semi-circle. Millie's cabin mate and co-worker was showing them how to play a large, interactive video game. She stood off to the side and listened.

Satisfied that Danielle was not getting into trouble, at least for the moment, Millie slipped out the door and headed to Ocean Treasures, one of the ship's gift shops, which was located on deck seven, to check in on her friend, Cat Wellington.

Millie gazed in the large picture window and caught a glimpse of Cat's beehive hairdo, piled high atop her head. Ocean Treasures was closed and wouldn't open until the ship was in international waters. She tapped on the double glass door in the front.

Cat held up a finger and then darted to the door, unlocking it to let Millie slip inside. "Well? Did your family make it onboard?"

Millie nodded. "Yep. They're upstairs on lido at the sail away party. I'm going to give them a tour of the ship." She leaned her hip against the door and studied her friend's pale face. "Have you been sleeping any better lately?"

Cat shook her head. "No," she confessed. "Not really."

Millie patted her arm, a concerned expression etched on her own face. "I know you're still struggling with Jay's prison escape and I want you to know I'm here if you want to talk."

"Thanks. I appreciate that." Cat unlocked the entrance door to let Millie out and Millie turned back. "Are you getting off in San Juan?"

"I-I have the day off but no, I'm not." Cat lowered her gaze and shifted her stance. "I...don't need anything onshore so I've decided to stay on the ship."

Millie frowned. Ever since Cat's husband, Jay, had kidnapped and attacked her, her friend had refused to leave the safety and security of the ship.

At first, Millie thought all she needed was a little time to put the incident behind her. She had even offered to accompany her friend off the ship but Cat had dug in her heels and refused even to consider it.

Millie started to say something and then changed her mind, instead deciding to discuss it with their friend, Annette.

"I'll see you later," Millie said as she stepped into the hall and headed toward the galley.

Annette's kitchen area was not far from the gift shop and on the same deck.

Millie peeked through the round galley window and then gently pushed on the door to let herself in. She gazed around the large, open kitchen and prep area.

Amit, Annette's right hand man, was near the dessert station and he waved a spatula in her direction. "Miss Annette is in the storage room."

"Thanks Amit." Millie strolled between two large stainless steel prep stations and made her way to the expansive storage area in the back. "Knock-knock."

Annette Delacroix spun around, clipboard in hand. "Hey there. I was wondering how you were doing. How's the fam?"

"Great. I'm giving them the grand tour shortly," Millie said. "I'll bring them by to meet you."

Annette smiled and set the clipboard on top of a row of canned stewed tomatoes. "I can hardly wait."

"Seems we're going to have a few extra security guards onboard for this cruise," Millie told her friend.

"Oh really. Why?"

Millie repeated her story of the men in suits, Nikki taking them to meet the captain and Andy's statement about the extra security.

Annette stuck her hand on her hip. "That's odd. I wonder what is going on."

"Me too. I'm on my way to see Captain Armati next," Millie said.

"Ah." Annette lowered her eyelids and batted her eyes. "I'm sure he's anxious to see you."

Millie's face reddened. There had been sparks flying between Captain Armati and Millie, and they had even gone on a day date while in Jamaica, not long before he took his leave.

She hadn't heard from him since he left, which wasn't unusual. Contact with the outside world was limited – and expensive – while onboard the ship. The crew was allotted a certain amount of internet time each week, which Millie used up when she went through her emails and checked her bank account.

On occasion, if Millie had some hours off while in port, she would leave the ship in search of free Wi-Fi on the islands. The younger crewmembers were not only familiar with the free hotspots but also a wealth of information when it came to island communication.

Millie kept in touch with her children, especially her daughter, Beth, on a weekly basis, and her son, Blake, but on a more limited basis. Blake wasn't much of a phone person and last time she'd talk to Beth, her daughter had mentioned Blake had just broken up with his girlfriend. The relationship had been short-lived and Millie hadn't even met her.

The holidays had passed and although Millie had been a little sad to be alone, she had Annette and Cat to keep her company. The three of them had celebrated together, along with Andy and Amit.

Siren of the Seas had been decorated in festive Christmas decorations and holiday music played throughout the ship, but it was still a hard for Millie to see all the happy families spending time together for the holidays while she was without hers.

It had been the first Thanksgiving and Christmas Millie had ever been away from home and family. It was a good thing she had stayed busy.

Millie started to go and then remembered Cat. "Cat isn't getting off in San Juan, although she has the day off."

Annette frowned. "Oh no. That no-good thug ex of hers is still controlling poor Cat, even from a prison cell thousands of miles away."

"We need to do something about it. I'm worried about her," Millie said. "The longer she refuses to face her fears, the harder it will be for her to move past the incident and get on with her life."

Millie understood Cat's fears were well founded. Jay, her ex, had escaped from prison and tracked Cat down while Siren of the Seas was docked at a remote island and then kidnapped her...with one goal in mind...to torture and kill his ex-wife.

"Maybe we can talk to her later," Millie suggested and then changed the subject. "I better get going if I want to stop by the bridge before meeting Gloria and Liz up on deck."

"I'll be back with them for the grand tour," Millie promised as she stepped out of the storage pantry and made her way through the kitchen and out into the hall.

***

Meanwhile, back on the panorama deck...

Gloria Kennedy knocked on the door that connected Andrea, Lucy and her suite to Margaret, Dot and Ruth's.

The door opened and Ruth peeked around the corner.

"You want to leave these doors open?" Gloria asked.

"Sure, why not." Dot swung the door open. Gloria crossed the threshold and stepped into the room. She hadn't been inside their suite yet and wondered if the layout was the same, which it was.

Margaret was lying on a lounge chair out on the balcony sunbathing. She shaded her eyes and peered into the room. "C'mon in. Join the party."

Meanwhile, Ruth was standing on a sofa gazing up at a small vent in the ceiling. She glanced at Gloria and turned her attention back to the vent cover. "I wonder how hard it would be to set up surveillance inside there."

"You're not considering bugging this place..." Gloria's voice trailed off.

"No, of course not." Ruth stuck a hand on her hip. "That would be crazy." She hopped off the sofa. "Did you happen to notice all the surveillance cameras onboard the ship? They're everywhere!"

Gloria hadn't noticed. She doubted 99% of the passengers onboard had noticed, but most passengers weren't her friend, Ruth, who had an extreme obsession with spy equipment, which had come in handy during several of Gloria's investigations in and around their small town of Belhaven, Michigan.

"I'm going to join Margaret on the balcony." Andrea made her way into the suite wearing a baby blue tank top and matching blue shorts.

The girls' adjoining balcony was spacious and boasted several chaise lounge chairs. Next to the chairs were small tables.

Lucy wandered into the suite. She flopped down on the small sofa, grabbed the cruise ships' travel guide and flipped through the pages. "Wow! There are some cool islands. Look at the gorgeous, turquoise waters. Can we go kayaking?"

Gloria grinned. This cruise had been Lucy's brainchild. She was the instigator and had planned the entire cruise.

The trip had been on Lucy's bucket list for several years, and she had been so excited when she found out Gloria and Margaret had booked the cruise as a surprise for all of them. "I'll try it, Lucy."

"Someone is knocking on your door." Dot stuck her head into Gloria's suite. She disappeared inside the room and returned with Liz and Frances in tow.

Liz was carrying a plate of assorted vegetables and a container of vegetable dip.

Frances was behind her, carrying a plate of cookies, which she set on the small coffee table, right in front of Lucy.

"Where did you get those?" Lucy reached for a chocolate chip cookie.

"Room service." Liz slid the plate of veggies and dip next to the cookies. "Did you know we have twenty four hour room service?"

They had eaten just a couple hours earlier, right before the mandatory safety drill. "We ate not two hours ago," Gloria pointed out.

Liz reached for a carrot stick. "So? I plan to get my money's worth."

The girls chatted about the ship, the port stop in San Juan the following day, and what time they would meet for dinner as they munched on the treats.

"What should we do now?" Liz looked at her watch.

Margaret emerged from the balcony. "I'm ready for one of those tall, frosty frozen concoctions with a little umbrella sticking out of the top."

"Sounds good to me," Ruth said.

Andrea, who had followed Margaret inside, nodded. "I could use something to cool me off."

The girls closed the balcony doors, gathered their keycards and headed to the lido deck.

***

Millie picked up the pace and headed toward the stairs as she made her way to the bridge. She reached deck ten, made a hard right and rounded the corner. The entrance to the bridge was at the end of a small hall.

Millie slipped her lanyard from around her neck and swiped her access card through the slot. The light blinked green, and Millie turned the handle to let herself in.

She had only visited the bridge a couple times while Captain Armati was on leave. She stepped inside and glanced around. Nothing had changed since her last visit.

Her eyes were drawn to the front of the ship and the wall of windows. The expansive ocean view never ceased to amaze Millie. It was magnificent. The captain and crew had the best view onboard Siren of the Seas.

She shifted her gaze to Captain Armati, who stood off in the corner, his back to her as he talked to Antonio Vitale, the staff captain.

Millie cleared her throat and the captain spun around, a serious expression on his face. When he saw Millie, he lifted a brow and the frown vanished, replaced with a wide grin. "Ah, Millie! I was wondering if you would stop by."

Captain Vitale nodded at Millie, grabbed a pair of binoculars and turned his attention to the open waters.

"Come." Captain Armati waved her toward the small hall that connected the bridge and his private quarters. "Scout will be thrilled to see you!" He punched in his access code and when the door beeped, he pushed it open and stepped aside so Millie could enter.

"Scout," Millie called out. "Where are you?"

A small brown ball of fur came barreling across the room and crashed into her ankle. The teacup Yorkie danced in a circle, let out a small whine and then began pawing at her leg.

Millie bent down, picked him up and cuddled him close. "Look at you. Did you miss me?"

She laughed as he licked her face and then placed his paw on her cheek.

Captain Armati closed the door behind them and they stepped into his living room. "The first thing he did when we got here was search the entire apartment. I believe he was looking for you."

Scout wiggled and squirmed until finally, Millie set him on the floor. He darted over to his pile of toys, pulled out a stuffed monkey, carried it over to her and dropped it on her foot.

"For me?" She leaned over and picked it up as she patted his head before standing up.

Captain Armati took a step closer, so close Millie's pulse began to race. She caught of whiff of his cologne, a mixture of woodsy and masculine.

"We both missed you." His brooding dark eyes met hers and a rush of warmth flooded her body.

"I missed you too," she whispered. He was close now, so close she could feel his warm breath on her cheek. He reached up and placed the palm of his hand on the side of her face, leaned in and softly kissed her lips.

Millie closed her eyes and held her breath, lost in the moment. Finally, he pulled back leaving her breathless and lightheaded.

"Perhaps you would like to join me here for dinner tomorrow night?" he suggested.

"Tomorrow night?" Millie drew a blank. The kiss had taken every ounce of sanity from her head. "Yes-yes. I would love that," she stammered.

37

"Good. It's a date. Six o'clock here in my cabin." He smiled and the solemn expression reappeared. "Andy said you have family onboard."

"Yes. Two of my cousins and their friends. In fact, I should get going. I promised to give them a tour of the ship."

Captain Armati led her to the door, reached for the handle and then paused. "It is good to be back."

"It's good to have you back," Millie softly replied.

She nodded to Captain Vitale as she followed Captain Armati to the exit. Her face still felt flushed and she wondered if Captain Vitale had noticed.

The captain held the door for Millie. "I shall see you tomorrow then."

She smiled and floated out the door, almost running smack dab into a brick wall...a formidable man with cropped hair and a frown on his face.

"I'm sorry." Millie shifted to the side. The stranger, who never bothered acknowledging her presence, strode into the bridge and slammed the door in her face.

Chapter Three

"How rude!" Millie stared at the closed door and wondered if he was one of the extra security guards Andy had mentioned. Her gut told her he was. She would have given anything to be a fly on the wall and listen in on the conversation on the other side of the closed door.

When she reached the tiki bar on the lido deck, Gloria, Liz and their friends were all waiting at the bar.

Millie smiled and pointed at the frozen peachy-orange concoction inside one of the tall, frosted glasses. "That looks interesting. What is it?"

Margaret held it up. "The drink is called 'Frosty Lips,' made with peach schnapps, mango mix and grenadine. It's delicious. Do you want to taste it?"

Millie took a step back. "No thanks. No drinking on the job."

"We tried to order Margaret a few shots of moonshine but they didn't have any," Gloria quipped.

Margaret gave her a dark look while the others chuckled.

"Hmm?" Millie raised a brow.

"Sorry. It's an inside joke," Gloria said and then changed the subject. "We're ready for the tour."

"Great! Let's go!" Millie waved them forward and they headed to deck fifteen, the spa deck, where they toured the tranquility area, one of three separate spa areas along with a VIP lounge for diamond guests. "Since you're suite guests, you have access to the VIP lounge during happy hour. It opens at five and closes at seven thirty. They serve a variety of drinks, both alcoholic and non-alcoholic, along with scrumptious hors d'oeuvres, straight out of the executive chef's kitchen."

Millie continued the tour through the rest of the ship, working her way down until they finished on deck two where medical and security were located.

She stood in front of the frosted glass door leading to the medical center. "Hopefully, none of you will need to see Doctor Gundervan while onboard."

The last stop was security and she stepped to the side. "Hopefully, you won't need to see our Head of Security, Dave Patterson, either."

"I read somewhere there are holding cells onboard cruise ships," Liz blurted out.

Millie nodded. "Yes. There are on Siren of the Seas, as well. You don't want to end up there."

"If anyone ends up in the hoosegow during this trip, it'll be Gloria," Ruth remarked.

Gloria frowned at her friend.

The door to the security office swung open and two tall, blonde-haired men Millie had never seen before stepped out. Following the men was a somber Dave Patterson.

The women shifted back to move out of the way.

Millie watched the men walk down the long hall, their shoes clicking on the smooth surface.

Dave Patterson waited until they were out of earshot and then turned to Millie. "Hello Millie. What brings you to my neck of the woods?"

"I'm giving my cousins and their friends a tour of the ship. I thought I would bring them by medical and show them where security was located."

Patterson shoved his hands in his pockets and rocked back on his heels. "Did you show them lock up?" he teased.

"No." Millie frowned, "but I told them where it was."

"I would like to see it," Lucy piped up.

Millie glanced at Dave Patterson, who shrugged his shoulders. "Okay by me. It's empty right now."

"It's not much to look at." Millie removed her lanyard from around her neck, swiped the slot on the front of the door and then entered the four-digit access code on the keypad. The ship had recently changed its' policy and staff and crew now needed not only a special access card, but also a four-digit code to enter the ship's temporary holding area.

Dave Patterson opened the door and held it for the girls. Millie had been in there briefly awhile back. She avoided the area whenever possible due to the small, enclosed space, which caused her to feel claustrophobic.

The small cells consisted of floor-to-ceiling bars and on the ceiling were tangled webs of thick, metal pipes that made an eerie clanging noise.

Millie shivered. The place gave her the creeps. "That's it ladies. Not much to look at." She stepped into the hall and the girls followed her out.

Dave Patterson closed the door behind them and then tugged on the handle to make sure it had locked.

"I heard they have a place to keep bodies if someone onboard dies," Liz said.

"There is," Millie replied. "It's back there." She pointed to the end of the hall, past Dave Patterson's office.

"Wow! All the good stuff is on this floor," Andrea said as they made their way to the stairs and the other end of the ship.

Dave Patterson grabbed the handrail and took a step up. "It was a pleasure meeting you, ladies. Enjoy your cruise."

Millie and the girls headed down one deck to the crew quarters where she showed them the crew dining area as well as the activity room and bar before leading them down the hall to the cabin she shared with Danielle.

Millie swiped her card through the slot, opened the door and nearly collided with Danielle, who was on her way out.

"Millie!" Danielle's eyes slid to the women standing behind Millie. "This is your family I take it?"

Millie introduced the women, with a little help from Gloria since Millie still didn't have all their names straight yet. When she got to Andrea Malone, the youngest one in the group, the women paused.

Danielle and Andrea could have been sisters. Their hair was the same shade of blonde and they wore it in a similar style. They were also almost the same height.

Danielle may have been a couple years younger.

Gloria stepped forward and gazed at Danielle. "Amazing. You two look a lot alike."

The blonde women studied one another, as if sizing the other up.

Danielle was the first to look away. She turned to Millie. "You see those stiffs earlier in the suits? I can spot G-men from a mile away."

"G-men?" Millie lifted a brow.

"You know. FBI. Federal agents. I would bet a hundred bucks that's what they were. Heard they went up to the bridge and had some sort of closed door meeting with the captain."

Millie was certain that tidbit of information had spread like wildfire and most of the staff and crew onboard had heard the same thing. "What do you think they were doing?"

Danielle had worked as an undercover agent with and around federal agents for several years before taking a position onboard Siren of the Seas as one of the entertainment staff.

Millie knew she was gunning for a position in the security department, but so far, nothing had opened up so she was stuck where she was at...and Millie was stuck with her for who knew how long.

Danielle had a knack for getting into a bind and Millie had already saved her neck, literally, twice now. She was a real pain in the rear without even trying to be.

The young woman crossed her arms and leaned against the wall. "It has to be something big. I mean, they don't send G-men out for every day criminal activity. If I had to guess, the feds have reason to believe something is about to go down and it has something to do with this ship."

Millie remembered what Andy had told her about extra temporary security on board for the voyage. Could it be they had something to do with the feds' visit? She opened her mouth to tell them what Andy had said but remembered that it was supposed to remain hush-hush and quickly closed it.

On top of that, she didn't want to frighten Gloria, Liz and their friends. Instead, she decided to have a pow wow with Annette and Cat to tell them what Danielle had said.

Millie accompanied Gloria, Liz and their friends back to their suites where they planned to hang out until dinnertime. They told Millie after dinner they were going to the theater to watch the evening headliner.

The following day, the first full day of the cruise, was a port day. The ship planned to stop in San Juan, Puerto Rico where the girls had decided to tour the fort, Castillo San Felipe del Morro in Old San Juan, located not far from the port.

After a tour of the fort, they would wander over to Old San Juan for a walking tour and then do a little shopping before heading back to the ship in time for the late afternoon departure.

Before she left, Millie reminded them to make sure they took their passports and key cards with them when they left the ship and to make sure they stayed on ship time.

Siren of the Seas had recently changed itineraries and this would be the third time the ship had stopped in San Juan. Millie was scheduled to work the following day and wouldn't have time to get off the ship, which was fine with her.

She'd already toured the old fort and city and would rather save her day off for one of the other ports like St. Thomas or St. Croix, the other two islands the ship would be visiting during this voyage.

Millie found Annette in the galley piping frosting on a cake. "I thought you were going to stop by with your cousins," Annette said as she squeezed the end of the bag.

"We did," Millie said. "Suri told me you had just taken a break. We missed you by a few minutes." She pulled a barstool from the corner of the room and hopped up on it as she watched her friend.

"I can see the wheels spinning," Annette teased. "What's going on?"

"Before the ship left, a couple men in suits met with the captain in the bridge. Danielle said she thinks the men in the suits were federal agents and that something big is going on."

Annette placed the frosting bag next to the cake. "You don't say. Yeah. Sounds about right. Could be anything. Maybe they're after someone, serial killer, mobster, a spy. Or maybe they're after a drug trafficking ring...flushing out a terrorist plot. Who knows?"

Millie shifted on the barstool. Several people onboard the ship knew who those men were and why they had boarded the ship – Captain Armati, Purser Donovan Sweeney and Dave Patterson, Head of Security. If only there was some way she could get one of them to slip up and spill the beans.

"I'm gonna grab a bite to eat before I have to report to work." She hopped off the barstool and slid it back in the spot where she'd found it. "Maybe if we all keep our ears to the ground we can figure out what the heck is going on."

Millie stopped by to chat with Cat at the gift shop, which was full of shoppers. She briefly told her what she knew before heading to the crew dining area to eat a bowl of unidentifiable stew, a mixture of shredded beef, mushy carrots and potato wedges mixed in with some peas.

She gobbled her dinner, and then headed out of the crew dining room where she ran into Danielle in the hall.

"I've been looking for you," Danielle whispered under her breath. "Andy is fit to be tied. Someone broke into his cabin and tore the place apart."

Chapter Four

"What the heck!" Millie, along with Danielle, raced down the hall to the other end of the ship where Andy's cabin was located. When they got there, the door was wide open and Andy was inside, pacing back and forth while he shouted into the phone. "I want security down here pronto! I don't care if you're having a meeting with the president. Someone broke into my cabin and trashed the place!"

Millie took a hesitant step forward and looked around. He was right. The place looked like a tornado had touched down.

Busted picture frames littered his small desk. The sofa cushions had been crammed into the small space between the arm of the couch and the wall.

The door to the mini fridge was wide open, and there were unopened soda cans scattered across the floor.

Andy's closet doors were also wide open. Millie craned her neck to peek inside the open doors. "Oh my gosh!" Millie gasped. The hangers were all empty and Andy's clothes, including his work clothes, lay in a haphazard heap on the closet floor.

Andy hung up the phone. "You should see my bathroom," he said. "Someone broke in here, obviously looking for something."

"I came down as soon as I heard." Dave Patterson, accompanied by Oscar, Patterson's second in command, stepped into the cabin. He slowly gazed around the room as he surveyed the mess. "You touch anything?"

"Only the phone to call security, since you wouldn't answer on the two-way radio," Andy replied.

Patterson turned to Millie. She lifted her hands. "Don't look at me. I just got here."

"Me too," Danielle added.

Dave Patterson and Oscar carefully surveyed the damage. "Do you want to stay while we investigate?" Patterson asked Andy.

"Yes!" Andy nodded and turned to Millie. "You're gonna have to fill in for me. The first headliner show starts in half an hour."

Millie swallowed hard. Although she loved her job, she hated to host the theater shows...all those passengers...hundreds, if not thousands of them, staring at her. Last time, she'd had to open for a show she'd suffered a severe case of stage fright.

If Zack, one of the dancers, hadn't pushed her onto the stage, she would've turned tail and bolted.

The palms of her hands grew sweaty at the thought. "I..."

"I'll do it," Danielle offered. "No biggie."

Millie thought that sounded like an excellent idea but Andy was not having it. "Millie," he warned.

"Okay! But if I pass out and embarrass myself, I'll never forgive you," she threatened. She stomped out of the cabin and into the hall.

Danielle followed behind her and fell into step as Millie marched down the hall. "You'll do fine. Don't worry. Just pretend they're all naked."

"It doesn't work," Millie muttered. "I've tried that before."

The theater was already starting to fill up when the two women made their way down the center aisle and to the back.

Millie began to pace back and forth behind the large, velvet theater curtains.

The echo of voices grew louder as the theater filled.

Alison Coulter, one of the dancers who had been in the dressing room getting ready for the show, made her way over. "What's wrong Millie? You look stressed out."

"Andy is dealing with a small crisis and Millie has to fill in," Danielle explained.

"Oh." She held out her arm to stop Millie's pacing. "Let's try some breathing exercises to calm you. It works like a charm for me."

Millie focused her attention on Alison. "Okay."

Alison lowered her voice. "Breathe in and...hold it. Close your eyes. Visualize softly swaying palm trees and the sound of waves washing onto a white sandy beach."

Millie sucked in a breath and closed her eyes.

"Now slowly breathe out...," Alison said in a soft, soothing voice.

Millie began to feel lightheaded. She tilted to the side and began to topple over.

A quick moving Danielle caught her. "Easy does it." She helped Millie into a chair near the side of the stage.

Danielle picked up a stack of papers from a table nearby and began to fan Millie's face. "This isn't going to work."

Alison knelt down and patted Millie's cold, clammy hand. "What if Danielle went with you? You could make it a co-emcee introduction."

Millie lifted her head and opened her eyes. It was a thought. Andy hadn't said Millie had to go it alone. She gazed at Danielle. "Will you?"

"Absolutely." Danielle nodded as the orchestra began the introduction piece, signaling it was time for Andy...Millie to make an appearance and announce the show.

"Here goes nothing." Millie scooted out of the chair and stood.

Danielle grabbed Millie's elbow and propelled her forward.

Felix, another dancer, handed each of them a mic and mouthed the words "hot mic." The microphones were on.

Millie plastered a smile across her face and the women strolled center stage. "Good evening ladies and gentlemen," Millie said.

"Welcome to Siren of the Seas. We trust you're all having a wonderful vacation so far," Danielle chimed in.

The two women bantered back and forth and Danielle's presence helped put Millie at ease. Before she knew it, the orchestra music picked up, their cue that their part was over and the show was about to start.

The girls wrapped up their introduction and exited stage left.

As soon as they were behind the edge of the curtain and out of sight, Millie collapsed against the wall and clutched her chest dramatically. "Holy smokes. I should get a raise for my performance," she gasped.

"Me too," Danielle grinned. "You did great." The women turned their attention to the show. After the show ended, they made sure the stage costumes, all the way down to the last feathered headpiece, had been put away.

Finally, Millie was able to relax. It had been a long day and an even longer evening.

Tomorrow would be another busy day and she was exhausted. "I think I'll turn in," she told Danielle as she turned off the theater lights. "I have a feeling tomorrow is going to be crazy."

Little did Millie know how true that statement would be.

***

Millie's eyes flew open and she sat straight up in bed. It was pitch black inside the cabin. "Danielle?"

Nothing.

She flung the covers back and crawled out of bed. "Danielle, are you in here?"

Silence.

Millie shuffled across the room. Seven shuffles. She had it down to a science. It was seven steps from the edge of her bunk to the bathroom door.

She fumbled for the door handle and pulled it open. Millie flipped the bathroom light switch and peered at the top bunk. It was empty.

Danielle, typically not an early riser, was already gone. She glanced at the small wall clock above the bathroom towel rack. Six forty-five a.m. The girls' daily schedule typically started at seven thirty when they had to report to Andy's office. Perhaps Andy had sent Danielle to check on the early risers' yoga class in the gym.

Inside the small bathroom, she could feel the ship shudder as it docked in the Port of San Juan. If Millie hurried, she would have enough time to grab a quick bite to eat before reporting to work.

Millie flew through her morning ritual as she took a quick shower, pulled her hair back in a

61

messy bun, and dabbed a little foundation and mascara on before slipping into her work uniform and heading to the crew dining room.

The place was packed. Millie joined the long line off to the side of the buffet area.

The line moved quickly, unlike Waves, the buffet area for passengers, where it seemed to take forever to make it through the food line. The crewmembers were on a tight schedule and didn't have time to lollygag.

She grabbed a couple pieces of soggy wheat toast, some watery scrambled eggs and something that slightly resembled sausage patties. The last thing she placed on her tray was a cup of coffee before she cautiously turned to search the dining area for an empty seat.

Millie spotted Nikki and Sarah, her former roommate, off in the corner. Sarah waved her over and pointed to an empty chair at their table.

Millie shuffled to the table and slid her tray on top before pulling out the chair and plopping down.

Sarah eyed Millie's plate of food. "The eggs are gross. You're gonna need a lot of salt and pepper to doctor them up."

"Thanks for the tip." Millie grabbed the saltshaker and shook some on top of the eggs before spreading a spoonful along the center of her limp toast. She folded it in half and took a bite. "Did you ever find out what the suits were doing in the bridge?"

Nikki shook her head. "Nope, but I can tell you some of the security guys have been hanging around the atrium. It's weird. We hardly ever see them in our area. There's also this other guy who keeps hanging around. He doesn't look like security, though."

"I better go." Nikki glanced at her watch, pushed back her chair and reached for her tray. "Should be a busy port day."

"Yeah, I have to go too." Sarah shoved her chair back and reached for her tray. "See you later."

Sarah followed Nikki to the exit where the girls dropped their dirty dishes in the bins and disappeared from sight.

Millie quickly finished her breakfast and headed to Andy's office, anxious to find out if security had figured out who had broken into Andy's cabin and why.

Chapter Five

Millie stepped inside the dark theater. As she got close to the stage, she could hear the sound of voices. She hurried up the steps and made her way to Andy's small office located in the back.

Danielle was already there and seated next to Andy. Their heads were close together, as they spoke in low voices.

Millie cleared her throat. "Ahem."

Andy's head shot up. "Millie! We were just talking about you." He waved her to the seat on the other side, directly across from Danielle.

"I heard you two did a bang-up job last night for the first show intro," he said.

"Thanks to Danielle." Millie gave credit where credit was due. She quickly changed the subject. "What happened last night after we left? Was Dave Patterson able to figure out who broke into your cabin?"

Andy's expression grew grim. "No. I heard this morning not only did someone break into my cabin, but they also tried to break into Donovan Sweeney's office."

Nikki's words echoed in the back of Millie's mind, how someone had been hanging around the guest services area. The door leading to Purser Donovan Sweeney's office was behind the guest services desk. Was the person Nikki noticed the same one who had tried to break in?

Millie made a mental note to stop by guest services and ask Nikki if she could keep an eye out for the man, to see if he was hanging around again today.

"...and she can handle bingo since there aren't any youth activities scheduled until the guests are back on board later today."

Millie pulled herself from her musings and tried to focus on Andy's words. "What will I do?"

Andy leaned back in his chair and crossed his arms. "I already told you while you were a million miles away. What's going on in that head of yours, Millie?"

Millie shifted in her chair and glanced at Danielle. "Well, I've been thinking...the suits that came onboard yesterday; Nikki Tan said she escorted them to the bridge. You said there were some extra security guards onboard for this cruise. Nikki said this morning security was hanging around the atrium. Last night someone broke into your cabin and tried to break into Donovan Sweeney's office."

She went on. "Something is going on, that's all. I'm just curious."

"Whatever it is, it's none of our concern, Millie. We need to focus on doing our jobs. If there is something going on, let security handle it."

He turned the conversation to the day's schedule. "You and I are going to the gangway to assist the first wave of passengers disembarking for the day. After that, I would like you to help Alison and Tara with the line dancing class."

Andy slid Millie's schedule in front of her and she glanced at the sheet. It would be a full day, not that she minded. She shifted her gaze to the evening schedule and breathed a sigh of relief. Andy had given her a few hours off close to the dinner hour so she could have dinner with Captain Armati.

"Looks good." She started to fold the sheet in half when something caught her eye. "Acupuncture at two in the spa!"

"Thanks for reminding me." Andy tapped the end of his pen on top of his black book. "A few weeks ago we brought in a new company for this service. We received several complaints from our last round of guests on the acupuncture sessions so I want you to go in incognito for a treatment and report back."

Millie frowned. "It sounds painful. Can't you send Danielle instead? She likes pain."

Danielle kicked Millie under the table.

"Ouch!" Millie glared at her.

"Unfortunately, Danielle was in the area earlier for the Sunrise Stretch yoga class and I'm afraid the spa employees will recognize her. They haven't seen you yet."

"Plus I have a couple hours off," Danielle explained. "I'm going to get off the ship and head into Old San Juan."

"Danielle has some time off this afternoon. She reports back to work before the dinner hour and in time for trivia." Andy explained. "All you'll need to do is change into some street clothes and then run up there around two. They won't be busy since the majority of passengers will be off the ship. It shouldn't take long, may be fifteen or twenty minutes."

"Twenty minutes of torture, while someone sticks needles in my body?" Millie placed her fingers against her temples and began to rub.

She could feel a major migraine coming on. "What am I going to tell them I'm there for?"

Danielle lifted a hand to her mouth to hide her grin. "You could say you have stress and anxiety."

"Or are coming in for fertility," Andy teased.

Millie's eyes widened. "Fertility! As in having a baby?"

"I'm kidding," Andy said. "Tell them whatever you want." He slid a key card across the table. "You'll have to use this temporary guest card to pay," he explained.

Millie glanced at name on the card. "Doris Ficklebomb...*Doris Ficklebomb!* What kind of crazy name is that?"

Andy closed his planner, placed his pen on top and stood. "Don't let me down, Doris." He winked.

Millie popped out of her chair. "You owe me one!"

The trio strolled out of the office. Danielle headed upstairs to check the youth areas, and Andy and Millie headed to the gangway. They made it just in time for the first wave of passengers to exit the ship.

She caught a glimpse of Gloria and her entourage as they exited the ship, dressed for a day of island adventures.

"You should have dinner with them one evening," Andy suggested as they watched them leave.

"Good idea, but not tonight," she said.

Andy shifted his gaze. "Why? What's tonight?"

Millie's face reddened and she clamped her mouth shut.

"Ahh." Her boss slowly nodded his head. "Captain Armati invited you to dinner?" Andy correctly guessed.

Thankfully, a passenger approached, unsure of what she would need to get back on the ship and the conversation ended.

After the initial rush of passengers exited the ship, Millie headed upstairs and Andy headed to a meeting with Donovan Sweeney, Captain Armati and Dave Patterson. He swore it was a planned meeting and nothing out of the ordinary.

The lido deck was deserted. Millie passed Danielle on her way to the back of the ship and the adults-only pool area.

Siren of the Seas sister ship, Baroness of the Seas, was docked directly beside them, which was another reason Millie was glad she hadn't gotten off. San Juan would be packed with thousands of passengers descending on the small island.

The morning passed quickly and as the hours slipped by, Millie's dread over the acupuncture session grew. She hated needles!

At 1:45, she headed back to the cabin to change into a sleeveless blouse and shorts for her session. Her steps dragged as she exited the cabin and shuffled to the stairs. It felt as if she was making her way to her own execution. What if the acupuncturist was a crackpot and he scarred her for life?

Millie almost backed out but forced herself to climb the stairs to the spa deck. She made her way to reception desk and the woman who was standing behind the counter. "Yes. I'm Doris...Ficklebomb...and I have a two o'clock appointment for torture, I mean acupuncture."

The woman glanced at the page, her finger following the line of names. "Ah. Yes, Ms. Ficklebomb. The session lasts roughly thirty minutes and the cost is one hundred twenty-five dollars. You can leave a tip if you enjoyed the service."

Millie handed the woman her fake card. *Enjoyed the service? People actually tipped someone to cause them pain? What kind of sick profession was this?*

The woman swiped the card and handed it back, along with a copy of the receipt to sign. "You can hold this until after the session ends and then add the tip," she suggested.

Millie was gonna tip all right, depending on the level of pain she felt. The greater the pain, the greater the tip would be. If Andy was gonna make her do this, he was gonna pay, she determined.

The woman went on. "Dr. Stephen Chow will be right with you."

Millie shoved the card and receipt in her front pocket and began pacing the floor, still uncertain what she would tell the good doctor was wrong with her. She was leaning towards anxiety, which wasn't far from the truth. This whole acupuncture exercise had her extremely anxious.

"Ms. Ficklebomb?" A man wearing a white lab coat and holding a clipboard stood next to the reception desk.

"Yes." Millie's armpits grew damp and a wave of fear coursed through her body.

"Follow me." The man motioned her to the back.

Millie took one last longing glance behind her. *What in the world had she gotten herself into?*

Dr. Chow stopped in front of an open door and waved her in. Inside the room was an examination table. In the corner was a small counter and on each side of the counter, a chair. Millie sidestepped the table and headed to the chair.

The doctor closed the door behind them. "I have a few questions before we begin."

He clicked the end of the pen and settled into the other empty chair. After asking her several questions regarding her health and the reason for the visit, to which she almost answered that she had been forced against her will, he asked her to open her mouth and stick out her tongue.

Dr. Chow turned on his pen light and looked inside her mouth. "You appear to be in good health."

The doctor opened a cabinet drawer, reached inside and pulled out a box. Inside the box were several long needles. On the ends of the needles were colored caps. "We will only work on your facial nerves so if I could get you to make your way over to the examination table."

Millie reluctantly rose from her chair and approached the table. She climbed on the step and backed onto the end of the padded table.

"You'll be more comfortable if you lie down," Dr. Chow told her.

Millie eased onto her back, closed her eyes and began to pray. "Dear Lord. Please don't let this hurt."

A pinprick sensation on the corner of her left eye caused it to start twitching. It was quickly followed by a pinprick near her right eye. "How many needles are you using?"

"Only twelve." Dr. Chow's voice was close to her ear.

Only twelve? Millie swallowed the lump that had formed in her throat. *Only. Twelve.* It might as well have been a hundred!

"Sometimes I use twenty but we start with twelve this time. If the symptoms persist, you may have to come back and we will try more needles."

Come back? There was no way on God's green earth she was coming back for another round of this!

The sharp stinging, a sensation akin to a bee sting, continued as he inserted a needle above each eyebrow, under her nose, in the corners of her mouth, then her chin. He finished with needles on both sides of her cheeks and under both eyes.

Millie felt like a voodoo doll and Andy was the one inserting the needles.

"I want you to relax." Dr. Chow's voice was near her ear.

Millie didn't dare open her eyes, lest the pain, which had subsided somewhat, returned with a vengeance. She laid there and quietly plotted her revenge on her boss.

Two sharp, quick pains radiated from her forehead. "I'm just going to twirl these needles while we wait."

A flash of fire coursed through her forehead and quickly shifted to her mouth. The sensation moved around as Dr. Chow apparently decided to twirl *all* the needles.

Millie began contemplated bolting from the table and pulling the needles out herself when the good doctor spoke.

"I take them out now," Dr. Chow said.

She braced for more pain but it never came.

"We are done. You can open your eyes."

Millie's eyes opened and she stared at the ceiling before shifting to a sitting position.

"It may take a few hours for the acupuncture to begin to work," he said as he helped her from the table. "If you aren't feeling relief from your severe anxiety by the end of today, you can call the desk and make another appointment."

Over my dead body!

Dr. Chow walked Millie to the front counter, handed her papers to the receptionist and disappeared down the hall.

Millie pulled the receipt from her pocket. "Can I borrow your pen?" She smiled sweetly at the young woman behind the desk, certain that droplets of blood were dripping from her open wounds causing her to look like some sort of apocalypse zombie.

"Yes, of course." The woman handed her a pen.

Millie had forgotten her reading glasses. She squinted at the tip line, jotted down a twenty-five dollar tip and signed her "name," *Doris Ficklebomb.* She handed the receipt to the girl, who asked for her cabin number.

Millie drew a blank. "My cabin number?"

"Yes. We will send other papers to your cabin."

Millie blurted out the first number that popped into her head...Gloria's cabin number. "Eleven two one two."

As she headed out of the spa, she made a mental note to let Gloria know she might be getting something delivered to her room with the name Doris Ficklebomb, but first, she wanted to stop by the guest services desk to see if Nikki had spotted the stranger hanging around again today.

Chapter Six

Now that Millie's torture session had ended, she realized she was hungry and hadn't eaten since early morning when she'd wolfed down the dry toast, tasteless eggs and rubbery sausage disk.

She made a quick pass through the buffet where nothing caught her eye and headed to the grill station out on lido deck. The lines were short and only a few passengers were milling about.

Millie skipped the tray, grabbed a plate and started at the end. The aroma of sizzling burgers caused Millie's stomach to growl and she slid a burger patty, topped with lettuce and tomato onto her plate, right next to a large sesame seed bun.

The french fries looked crispy and fresh so she placed a small mound next to the burger and topped both the burger and the fries with melted cheese sauce.

Millie placed two chicken tenders on her plate, ladled a small amount of honey mustard dressing into a small plastic cup and eased the cup next to the tenders.

She strode over to an empty table for two next to the large ocean view windows and settled in. From where she was seated, Millie could see the deck layout of Baroness of the Seas, docked next to them. The ship was a couple years newer than Siren of the Seas and slightly larger.

Baroness of the Seas' lido deck was two decks up and a pool slide meandered along the side while strategically placed tiki bars surrounded the spacious pool area.

She wondered if someday she would get a chance to work on one of Majestic Cruise Lines' other ships. The thought of leaving Captain Armati and Scout, not to mention Annette, Cat and Andy, made her sad. Millie hoped not but knew from talking to other crew, there was a good chance it would happen.

She popped a cheesy fry in her mouth and chewed.

Soon, it would be time to head down to greet returning guests. The ship was scheduled to set sail at four o'clock. Millie planned to stop by her cousins' suites to check on them after heading to her own cabin to get ready for dinner with Captain Armati.

Her pulse quickened as she remembered the passionate kiss that made her toes curl. She wondered if he would kiss her again.

Her whole body warmed at the thought. She picked up a Cruise Ship Chronicles daily schedule someone had left behind and began to fan her face.

The deck grew crowded as returning passengers descended on the area to grab a bite to eat or settle in for a few hours of sun and take an afternoon dip in the pool.

Millie cleared her table, dropped her dirty dishes in the bin and headed down to guest services on deck five.

Apparently, everyone was eating because guest services was deader than a doornail.

Nikki Tan was behind the counter, talking on the phone. She waved Millie over and hung up the phone when she approached.

Nikki leaned forward. "The guy I told you about earlier...he's over there." She jerked her head and pointed to a corner of the room that contained a small sofa and two cushioned high back chairs.

Standing directly behind the sofa was a tall, dark haired man wearing a plain white t-shirt and black resort shorts. He was casing the crowd, as Millie would describe it. "He has been hanging around ever since I got here this morning."

"I'm going to go talk to him," Millie said impulsively. She marched over to the man, who

84

now had his back to her, and tapped him on the shoulder. "Hi."

The man spun around and peered down at Millie. He was tall...taller than he originally appeared. "I'm Millie Sanders, Assistant Cruise Director. You look lost. Can I help you find something?"

"I'm fine," he frowned. "Just waiting on a friend."

"I see..." Millie said. "I didn't catch your name."

"John. And you said your name was Millie?"

"Yes. Millie." Millie wasn't about to give up. "Did you visit San Juan today, John? It's a lovely island with an old historic fort and a beautiful, picturesque walking district."

"No. I didn't."

She waved a hand. "Personally, I think St. Thomas is enchanting, as well. They have a large shopping district right outside the port with great deals on jewelry."

Millie glanced at his hand. He wasn't wearing a wedding band, which didn't necessarily mean he wasn't married. An image of Roger, Millie's ex-husband, popped into her head and she quickly pushed it back out.

"I'll keep that in mind. Now if you'll excuse me." John sidestepped Millie, wound his way past the circular staircase leading to the upper deck and disappeared from sight.

Millie's shoulders slumped. The only thing she'd learned was his first name was John, if that was even his name. She had her doubts.

She made her way back to the guest services desk where Nikki stood watching. "Is there any way to check on guests with the first name John?"

Nikki scrunched her brows. "John? Yeah, there are probably at least a couple dozen." She shifted her gaze to the computer screen in front

86

of her and tapped the keys on the keyboard. "Close. There are forty-two passengers onboard the ship with the first name John."

"Well, that narrows it down," Millie grimaced and glanced at her watch. "I better head over to the gangway. I'm sure Andy is waiting for me."

"Oh!" Nikki stopped her. "I forgot to tell you. Darna stopped by here earlier. He got off the ship to use his phone near one of the hot spots and started talking to one of the crew from the other ship, Baroness of the Seas. He said the guy worked security and mentioned they had extra security on their sailing, as well, something the guy said had never happened before."

"You don't say." Millie scratched the corner of her eye and wondered if the needles Dr. Chow had used had been sterilized.

She leaned forward. "Does my face look funny - like I have puncture wounds?"

Nikki tilted her head and studied Millie's face. "No. I don't see anything. Why?"

87

"Never mind." Millie waved a hand. "It's a long story. Thanks for the info Nikki." She power walked across the atrium and made her way down to the gangway where Andy was already greeting guests.

He glanced at her out of the corner of his eye. "How did the acupuncture session go?"

"I spent the entire time plotting my revenge," Millie warned.

Andy snorted. "C'mon. It couldn't have been that bad."

A couple stopped by with questions and Millie waited until they wandered off before replying. "Doris Ficklebomb! What kind of name is that?"

A slow smile crept across Andy's face. "I didn't have much time to think about a name. It was the first one that popped into my head. So what did you think? Was the acupuncturist professional? Did he hit on you or ask you to take your clothes off?"

Millie's head whipped around. "Take my clothes off! Guests were asked to undress?"

"Only the women," Andy said.

"No, he did not." Millie tapped her foot on the floor and stewed over Andy's admission.

Millie caught a glimpse of the top of Danielle's head as she "dinged" her key card and made her way over. "Whew!" She draped her lanyard around her neck.

"Yeah! It's a scorcher out there," Millie agreed.

"No. Not that," Danielle said. "Getting through security to board the ship was ridiculous! Security was what I would imagine getting into Fort Knox would be like. I had to pass through three separate screenings."

"You're kidding," Andy said.

A triple screening to board wasn't just unusual...it was unheard of. Millie had gotten off in port plenty of times and the screening procedure to get back on was always the same. All she'd ever had to do was show her photo ID, along with her key card before being waved through.

When ship passengers – and crew - reached the entrance to the ship, they inserted their ship card into a machine while security checked the monitor to make sure the picture that popped up on the screen matched the card the person was using.

The last step in the process was when passengers were required to place all purchases, bags and purses on a conveyor belt where security scanned them for banned items.

Passengers could purchase alcohol while in port, but when they re-boarded, the alcohol was removed from their belongings. The crew then tagged the liquor with the passenger's name and cabin number. During the last evening of the cruise, the ship's crew would deliver the confiscated liquor to the passengers' cabins.

"You should see the line to get back onboard the ship. It stretches all the way down the dock." Danielle swiped her hand across her forehead. "I'm going to take a shower so I can get back to work before the boss fires me." She winked at Andy and headed to the bank of elevators.

"I want to see what Danielle is talking about." Millie headed to the gangway and stood near the entrance, peering out. Sure enough, the line to board stretched along the fence line. She couldn't see the end.

"They better pick up the pace if they want all the passengers back on board before we set sail," she told the security guard, who was standing near the gangway.

"Yes, Millie. It is a mess out there. Oscar stopped by to say the passengers outside the gates are growing impatient."

Millie couldn't blame them. It would be pure misery, standing in a long line with the sun beating down. She slowly wandered back to where Andy stood waiting.

First, there were the men who visited Captain Armati, and then there was the extra security staff.

She thought about the dark haired man, "John," who had been hovering near guest services, about Andy's cabin that had been broken into, the extra security to re-board the ship and last, but not least, Darna who had told Nikki that Baroness of the Seas had added extra security, as well.

The pieces were beginning to fall into place and they all pointed to one thing. Could it be the Siren of the Seas and even Baroness of the Seas, had received some sort of terror or hijacking threat?

Chapter Seven

"Terror threat?" Annette tapped the top of the galley prep area with her fingernails. "Like someone is going to blow up our ship?"

It sounded incredible, even to Millie. "I'm...not sure. I mean, think about it. Why are all the extra security and G-men, as Danielle called them, visiting Captain Armati before the ship set sail?"

"We don't know they were FBI," Cat pointed out. "It could be something else."

"Like what? Breaking up a drug ring or perhaps searching for one of the ten most wanted?" Millie asked. All of it seemed far-fetched. There was only one thing for sure...something was going on and they weren't alone. Perhaps it was fleet-wide.

"We need to keep our ears to the ground and our eyes peeled," Millie said. She glanced at her watch. It was getting late and she wanted to check in with her cousin, Gloria, before her dinner date with Captain Armati. "I gotta go. I have dinner plans."

"Ah!" Annette said. "Birthday dinner date with the captain?"

"Birthday dinner? It's Captain Armati's birthday?" Millie's eyes widened.

Annette nodded. "Yeah. I got a special request from the bridge for a cake for the captain. Said it was for his birthday. I just finished decorating it. When Amit gets back from break, he's going to take it up there. Said they wanted it there right after the ship set sail."

The ship had left port less than half an hour ago.

"He should be here any time," Annette said as she walked over to the large stainless steel refrigerator. She opened the door and pulled out a layered cake. "It's red velvet. I guess it's his favorite," she said.

Annette had done a wonderful job on the cake. It was a work of art.

Millie chewed her lower lip thoughtfully. She had no idea it was the captain's birthday! Should she get him a gift? What do you give the captain of a ship? Maybe she could buy him a gift certificate for a massage. "I gotta run!"

Millie bolted from the galley, darted down the long hall and raced to the spa. The same woman who had been behind the counter earlier watched her approach. She smiled when she spotted Millie and then scrunched her brow as she glanced at Millie's work uniform.

"Ms. Ficklebomb. Are you here to schedule another appointment?" she asked.

"No way!" Millie blurted out. "I mean, no. I'm not, but I would like to buy a massage package." She pulled out the temporary "Doris Ficklebomb" card and grinned evilly. It was payback time. "I'll take the most expensive massage package you have."

The woman tapped the keys on her keyboard. "That is a fifty minute deep tissue massage for two hundred fifty-five dollars."

"I'll take it." Millie handed the card to the woman. After the woman swiped the card, she handed the card, along with a receipt to Millie, who promptly scribbled in a fifty-dollar tip, signed the receipt and handed it back to the girl.

The girl placed a certificate on the counter and using her pen, circled a number at the bottom. "Have the guest call this number when they're ready to schedule the massage session."

"Great." Millie folded the certificate and tucked it into her front pocket along with the receipt and the card Andy had given her.

Millie smiled triumphantly as she strolled out of the spa area and made her way down to the crew deck. She couldn't wait to see the look on Andy's face when she handed the card and receipts to him.

***

Ruth flopped down on the bed. "How was I to know I wouldn't be allowed to bring a smoke detector spy camera onboard?"

The girls filed in the suite and Andrea closed the door behind them. "It wasn't a big deal. So we had to run back to town to return it."

"Can't you buy your spy equipment back home?" Gloria asked.

Ruth sat up. "Of course I can, but I didn't have to pay sales tax, which would've saved me a good twenty bucks."

"Twenty, schmenty," Margaret griped. She reached inside her fanny pack and pulled out her wallet. "Here's the twenty bucks for tax." She tossed a twenty-dollar bill on the bed next to Ruth.

Ruth reached for the bill. "It's the principle of the thing." She handed the twenty back to Margaret.

"I thought they were gonna take you to a Puerto Rican prison," Gloria joked, only half-kidding.

The security to board the ship had been borderline ridiculous and it had taken forever. Not only had security checked each of their passports four separate times, they had thoroughly searched each of their bags.

They'd had to pass through a body scanner and after Ruth's spy equipment was discovered, they had to do it all over again...all of them. It took over two hours to get back on the ship.

"At least with the extra security, we know our ship is safe." Andrea plopped down in a chair and kicked off her tennis shoes. "The fort was cool and so was the old city. I would go back there again."

Andrea had purchased a container of sofrito, a Puerto Rican spice, for Alice, along with a small hand-painted mask to hang on the wall in her library. The clerk had told her it would bring her good luck. So far, it hadn't worked!

"It's a good thing Liz wasn't with us," Margaret said.

Liz and Frances had gotten off the ship with Gloria and the girls, but quickly tired of walking and the women decided to head back to the ship. If Liz had had to wait in the long lines, she would have pitched a fit.

"You got that right," Gloria groaned. She eased onto the couch, lifted her leg and rubbed her shin.

"Is your leg bothering you?" Dot asked.

A few months back, while Gloria was on her honeymoon, she had broken her leg. The cast had come off a few weeks earlier and she was thrilled, but every once in a while, she felt an odd twinge of pain, especially when she did a lot of walking...like today. "Nah! It's okay. Just a little twinge."

"The fort was worth it," Gloria added.

Castillo de San Felipe del Morro, or *El Morro,* as the locals called it, was a 400 year-old walled fortress, once used to protect the island of Puerto Rico from invading colonies.

The fortress was located on the northern tip of the Island of San Juan, not far from the port and it had been a short walk from the cruise ship. The fort itself offered breathtaking views of the water and historic Old San Juan. Despite the discomfort, Gloria was glad they had taken the time to visit the fort.

Someone began pounding on the hall door and then the door flew open. Liz, followed by Frances, strolled inside. "Good! You're back. I made dinner reservations for all of us at The Vine."

Lucy settled in next to Gloria. "What time?"

"Six o'clock," Liz said. She glanced around the suite. "Wear something nice. Frances and I are going down to the lounge to listen to some piano music and will meet you in front of The Vine at six sharp." She turned on her heel and the whirlwind...Liz...was gone.

Ruth slid off the bed and headed to the bathroom. "Looks like we got our marching orders. I'll get ready first."

"I'll head to our room and get ready first, unless you want to," Lucy said to Gloria.

"Nah. You go ahead," Gloria said. "Andrea can go after you and I'll go last."

"We should head to the balcony to see if we can still catch a glimpse of the San Juan coastline." Dot, Margaret, Andrea and Gloria wandered out onto the balcony. Off in the distance, they were able to see the fort's watchtowers.

It had been fun visiting a new place and Gloria had enjoyed the day, but she wasn't sure she would return to San Juan anytime soon. She was looking forward to a new island and the next adventure.

Tap-tap. Gloria shifted her gaze. "I thought I heard someone knocking." She made her way into her suite and opened the outer door.

Millie was standing outside the door wearing a silky, black pantsuit, dressed to the nines.

"Wow! Look at you!" Gloria gave her a quick hug and then stepped back. "Where are you going all gussied up?"

Millie's cheeks reddened. "I have a...uh...dinner date."

Gloria knew all about Millie's nasty divorce from her first husband, Roger, how he had cheated on her with one of his clients. She was thrilled when she found out her cousin had gotten a job onboard the cruise ship – far away from rotten Roger.

"Anyone serious? Are you having dinner with Andy, your boss?" Gloria teased.

Millie burst out laughing. "No! It's not Andy. It's Captain Armati."

Gloria raised a brow. "Whew! You're not messing around." She patted her cousin's arm. "Good for you. Perhaps I can meet him before our cruise ends."

"Definitely." Millie nodded. "I just wondered how your day in San Juan went and wanted to stop by to ask if perhaps I could join you and the girls for dinner tomorrow night."

Andrea overheard part of the conversation and strolled over to the door. "We were detained at the security checkpoint because Ruth purchased some shiny new spy equipment and the security searched us all."

"Uh-oh." Millie frowned. "What kind of spy equipment?" Annette would be interested in that!

"It's a camera that looks like a smoke detector," Gloria explained. "She won't try that again."

"How is Liz?" Millie asked.

"Annoying," Gloria said. "Frances and she went down to the piano bar to wait for us. We have dinner reservations at The Vine."

"Excellent choice." Millie nodded. "I hope you're hungry. Speaking of that, I better go."

She started to leave and then turned back. "Tomorrow is a sea day and I'll have to work most of the day. How does dinner at six-thirty sound?" It would give her enough time to eat with the girls and then head back to help Andy with the second show.

"Perfect." Gloria gave her thumbs up. "It will be nice to sit down and catch up with you. I can't wait to hear about some of your adventures."

Millie turned to go and remembered 'Doris Ficklebomb.' She placed a hand on the door. "By the way, if you have some papers delivered to your room, addressed to a Doris Ficklebomb, you can toss them."

Gloria opened her mouth to ask who Doris Ficklebomb might be, but decided that perhaps she didn't want to know. "Sure." Gloria grinned.

She waited until Millie disappeared down the long corridor before she shut the door.

Andrea patted Gloria's shoulder. "I can't imagine what would happen if you two ended up in some sort of high seas exploit."

"Whew!" Gloria shook her head. "Me either!"

Andrea – and Gloria - didn't know it yet, but they were about to find out.

Chapter Eight

Millie fiddled with the corner of the birthday card she had purchased at the gift shop for Captain Armati...Nic. She had had a hard time picking one out, unsure if she should go with slightly mushy, hilariously funny or serious. She decided on a middle of the road card... one that was a little funny but also a little sentimental.

She hoped he would like her last minute gift...the spa massage.

Millie straightened her jacket, smoothed her hair and tapped lightly on the bridge door. When no one answered, she tried again. This time she tapped hard. There was still no answer.

Millie pulled her keycard from her pocket, swiped it through the slot and waited for the green light.

The light never lit so she twisted the handle. The door was locked. She tried swiping her card a second time. Again, there was no green light and the door wouldn't budge.

Millie pounded on the outside as alarm bells sounded in her head. She had visited the bridge many times and never in all those times had her key card not worked.

Had something happened? What if Captain Armati changed his mind and decided to reset the card access?

It was futile. No one was going to answer the door and let her in.

Millie, her shoulders slumped, turned on her heel and shuffled down the hall.

She climbed one flight of stairs and stepped out onto the open deck. When she reached the rail, she ran her hand along the top absentmindedly.

Had the captain forgotten about their dinner date? How could he forget? He had just invited her the day before!

She tapped the tip of his birthday card on the railing. What if the kiss the day before had been a test and now he thought she was a wanton woman...a floozy who was desperate to have a man in her life again? But he had been the one who initiated the kiss, not her!

Millie knew she was grasping at straws. Nothing was making sense.

She began walking aimlessly, her thoughts bouncing back and forth between the captain changing his mind and standing her up to thinking perhaps something was wrong.

Millie stopped abruptly when she realized she was standing outside the Sky Chapel, one of her favorite spots onboard the ship.

She opened the door and stepped into the quiet, dark sanctuary. Her eyes were drawn to the beautiful stained glass wall and the cross, front and center.

She shuffled to the front pew, eased onto the seat and clasped her hands tightly in her lap.

Perhaps it wasn't God's plan for Millie to love again. Maybe she was meant to be alone.

A tear trickled down Millie's cheek and she angrily swiped it away. *This is not the time for a pity party.*

A Bible verse popped into Millie's head, one she had memorized when she'd gone through the darkest days of her divorce from Roger:

He will wipe every tear from their eyes. There will be no more death or mourning or crying or pain, for the old order of things has passed away. Revelation 21:4 NIV

She sucked in a deep breath and blinked rapidly. Surely, there was some reason the captain had stood her up!

Millie jumped at the sound of Andy's voice booming over the ship's speakers. "Millie Sanders, please report to guest services."

Something about the tone of Andy's voice caught her attention. Millie abruptly stood and strode out of the sanctuary.

She picked up the pace as she headed down to deck five.

Andy was waiting for her – more like pacing the floor – when she reached the atrium. "Follow me." He waved Millie out the side doors.

"Have you seen the captain?" he asked as soon as they were alone.

"No." Millie shook her head. "He invited me to dinner at six but when I got there, the bridge door was locked and my keycard wouldn't work. I don't understand."

Andy pointed at the water. "We're not moving, Millie. The ship has stopped. I just spoke to Dave Patterson. No one is answering in the bridge and no one is answering the phones or door in the engine room."

Millie's hand flew to her chest. The news was a mixed blessing. Perhaps the captain hadn't stood her up, after all.

He went on. "We tried to call ship to shore but we can't get through. We're trying to use cell phones to reach shore but so far aren't able."

"I hoped you had talked to him." Andy's eyes scanned the horizon. "Something is going on."

"There you are." Purser Donovan Sweeney stepped out onto the deck and stopped on the other side of Andy. "Nikki said you two were out here." He turned to Millie. "Have you seen Captain Armati?"

Millie shook her head and told him the same thing she'd told Andy...that the captain had invited her to dinner in his apartment at six o'clock and when she got to the bridge, her keycard wouldn't work and no one answered the door.

"It's his birthday, too, although I didn't know it until Annette told me." She tapped the edge of his birthday card on the rail. "I got him a gift and everything." *Courtesy of Andy,* she silently added.

Andy stared at the card in Millie's hand. "It's not Captain Armati's birthday. His birthday is Christmas Eve. He was home and on leave for his birthday."

"But Annette...Annette was sending a birthday cake to the bridge because she received a special request."

Perhaps Annette had been confused. She went on. "I wish we could figure out what is going on in the bridge and the engine room. What about the cameras?"

After the last incident where someone went overboard near the VIP deck, Captain Armati and Dave Patterson agreed it was time to install extra cameras not only in some of the more isolated areas of the ship, but also the bridge, engine room and Purser Sweeney's office. "All but two of the ship's cameras are working. The ones outside the bridge and outside the engine room are not. We have maintenance checking on them now."

A sudden thought occurred to Millie. "There is a way to see into the bridge. Not the whole bridge but the part that hangs over the side. My cousin, Gloria, and her friends, their suite is near the front of the ship and one deck above the bridge. From their balcony, you can see the part of the bridge that sticks out."

"What suite are they in?" Andy asked.

"Panorama eleven two one something." Millie shrugged. "I'll know it when we get there." She led the way as the trio hurried along the outer deck and to the steps near the front of the ship.

When they stepped back inside, Purser Sweeney headed to the bank of elevators.

"No!" Millie said. "What if the elevators stop working?" It was a stretch, but the last thing Millie wanted was to be stuck inside an elevator.

"True." Donovan Sweeney, Andy and Millie climbed the stairs until they reached deck eleven.

The men followed Millie to the front of the ship and stopped in front of Gloria's suite. "This is it," she announced and then lightly tapped on the outer door. No one answered.

She lifted her hand to try again. "Oh! I completely forgot! They had dinner reservations at The Vine at six o'clock. They won't finish dinner for at least another hour."

Andy plucked his keycard from his pocket. "I hate to do this to your family, Millie, but we need to get out onto the balcony."

"Gloria won't mind." At least Millie *hoped* she wouldn't mind.

She stepped to the side and waited while Andy swiped his access card through the slot and opened the door.

One of the interior lights was on, along with the television, giving them enough light to cross the spacious suite and make their way to the balcony doors.

Andy unlocked the slider, slid it open and waited while Millie, followed Donovan Sweeney, stepped out onto the balcony.

"There." Millie leaned over the rail and pointed to the left. "That's the bridge."

Andy and Donovan stood next to Millie as they leaned over and peered down. They were able to make out a few blinking lights and slight movement inside the bridge.

"The windows are tinted so it's hard to see inside," Donovan said. "Too bad we can't scope out the other end of the bridge."

"We can," Millie said. "My other cousin, Liz, and her friend are in the cabin across the hall and at dinner, as well."

They stepped off the balcony and into the suite. "How many family members are on this cruise?" Donovan Sweeney asked.

"Just two. My cousins, Gloria and Liz, but they are cruising with friends." Millie did a mental calculation. "Six friends so a total of eight women."

Andy shook his head. "Whew! If they're anything like you, heaven help us."

Millie frowned. "I'll take that as a compliment."

Andy and she waited in the hall while Donovan swiped his access card and opened the door to Liz's suite. Bright lights illuminated the interior.

The place was a disaster. Piles of dirty dishes filled every inch of available space on the make-up counter.

A path of discarded clothes dotted the floor, as if the owner had changed and dropped what they were wearing wherever they happened to be standing.

Shopping bags covered the top of the coffee table while several more were crammed underneath. Scattered across the sofa and both beds was an array of magazines and paperback books.

"Holy smokes! Did someone break into this cabin, too?" Andy gasped.

Despite the gravity of the situation, Millie laughed. "No. My cousin, Liz, is somewhat of a slob. This is normal," she reassured him.

Millie tiptoed around the items strewn across the floor as she made her way to the balcony. She opened the door and stepped outside. Andy and Donovan followed her.

The trio leaned over the balcony and peered into the bridge. A movement caught Millie's eye. "I think I see either Captain Armati or Staff Captain Vitale."

Her eyes squinted as she watched the person gaze out the bridge window.

They all three watched in horror as someone came up behind the person, hit him in the back of the head and he crumpled to the floor.

Millie clutched her chest. "Did you see that? Someone just knocked out one of the captains!"

Purser Donovan Sweeney nodded grimly. "I did."

The attacker grasped the unconscious person under the arms and dragged him from sight.

"Houston, we have a problem," Andy said.

"What are you doing in here?" A woman's voice shrieked.

Millie spun around and looked inside the suite. It was Liz.

Millie eased past Andy and stepped into the room. "We needed to take a look at something out on the balcony."

"Oh." Liz's shoulders sagged like a deflated balloon. "I thought you were room service here to clean up this mess."

Gloria, Liz's sister, followed her inside and surveyed the room. "This place needs a bulldozer," she joked and then turned her attention to Millie. "There's not much to see at night unless you're looking into the bridge, which is pretty cool."

The look on Millie's face told Gloria that was exactly what they were doing.

Gloria's detective radar sprang into motion and she stepped out onto the balcony. "Is something going on? The girls and I walked to the back of the ship and noticed the ship is not moving. Has something happened?"

Millie glanced at Donovan uneasily. "Perhaps. We're not certain." Although watching someone whack one of the captains on the back of the head and then drag him from sight was a strong indicator of a problem.

The other girls crowded out onto the balcony and tried to catch a glimpse of the bridge. "We can go back to our balcony and check out the bridge," Lucy suggested.

"Good idea." The women headed out of Liz's disaster zone, across the hall and into Gloria's suite.

"We took the liberty of borrowing your balcony, too," Millie admitted as she trailed behind.

Gloria waved a hand. "No biggie. So what do you think has happened?" she asked eagerly as she leaned over the railing and looked down. "All I can see are a few blinking lights. I wish I had a set of binoculars."

Ruth followed the others to the balcony and stood near the doorway. "I've got a pair in my suitcase." She darted through the connecting door and into the suite she shared with Margaret and Dot, returning moments later with a pair of high tech binoculars.

"These babies can get a visual up to a mile away and have XTR technology with the capability to see through a UV shield of three to five."

"Impressive." Millie took the binoculars from Ruth, pressed the rubber eyecups to her eyes and adjusted the dial. With the aid of the binoculars, Millie was able to see the edge of computer equipment near the side of the bridge. She was also able to catch a glimpse of Ingrid Kozlov, one of the computer techs, who worked in the bridge.

For some unknown reason, Ingrid did not like Millie, although Millie had never actually talked to the woman. She suspected it had something to do with Ingrid having a thing for Captain Armati and the woman was jealous.

Millie followed Ingrid's jerky movements as she kept glancing at something to the left and out of sight. It was too dark to see clearly and Ingrid was too far away for Millie to study the expression on the woman's face.

Donovan Sweeney squeezed in. "Let me see." Millie handed him the binoculars.

Donovan lifted the binoculars and studied the bridge before shifting them and gazing out into the open water. "There's something out there in the water. See the light?"

Millie followed his gaze. Sure enough, there were several small dots of light off in the distance. They had cruised from Puerto Rico hours ago and would be too far away to see lights from the island.

Siren of the Seas was on course for the island of St. Croix, which was southeast of San Juan. After a port stop in St. Croix, they would head north to St. Thomas before sailing back to the Port of Miami.

Andy was familiar with this route and so was Donovan. "Do you think the lights are from the Vieques Island?" Andy asked.

"No. We passed the island already." Donovan lowered the binoculars. "I think it's someone else, possibly terr…"

Donovan shifted his gaze. "I don't know what it is," he said. "We may need to borrow your suite again, ladies. Dave Patterson and his men will want to check this out. I'm sorry for the inconvenience."

Gloria waved a hand. "No problem. Whatever we can do to help," she added.

"Thank you." Donovan handed the binoculars to Ruth and turned to Andy. "Let's track down Dave Patterson."

Andy nodded. "Millie, you'll have to cover for me one more night and announce the headliner show in the theater."

"Sure. I'll leave here in a moment and head straight down there." At least she was dressed for the occasion.

Andy followed Donovan to the door and then turned back. "For now passengers must not know a thing. We need to keep a tight lip."

Millie made a zipping motion across her lips. "Yes sir!"

The door closed behind the men.

"He was going to say terrorists!" Gloria blurted out after the door shut behind them.

Chapter Nine

Millie slumped into the desk chair and stared at the door. She was thinking the exact same thing. Donovan was going to say the word "terrorist."

Donovan Sweeney had a closed door meeting with Captain Armati the day before the ship set sail. Captain Armati had shared confidential information with Donovan. Had the captain told him why there was extra security on board and why there was extra security checking passengers and crew before being allowed to re-board the ship in San Juan?

Millie thought about yesterday's break in of Andy's cabin and attempted break in of Donovan Sweeney's office.

Against her better judgment, Millie spilled the beans and told the girls all that had happened. She finished with the mysterious birthday cake delivery and then jumped out of the chair. "I've got to head down to host the Heart and Homes

Show. Maybe I can stop back later after my shift is over and we can put our heads together."

Gloria walked Millie to the door. "Absolutely." She waited for Millie to exit and then closed the door behind her. "I think it's time to do a little investigation of our own."

"I'm in," Ruth declared.

"Me too." Lucy rubbed her hands together.

"Sounds like a plan," Andrea nodded.

"I guess I better supervise," Margaret decided.

"No one is leaving me behind," Liz grumbled.

"Me either," Frances said.

"This won't end well," Dot predicted.

Gloria paced the floor. "We need to talk to Annette, the one who works in the galley, to find out what was up with the birthday cake and figure out if perhaps the cake was a ruse to allow someone to breach or access the bridge."

"I'm pretty sure I passed by the galley when I got lost earlier," Andrea said. "The galley is on the same floor as the gift shop."

The girls stepped out into the hall and followed behind Andrea as they headed to a bank of elevators.

"Stop!" Ruth blocked the elevator buttons with her hand. "If someone has managed to seize control of the ship, they may be able to control all the mechanicals, including the elevators."

"And the power supply, including lights," Gloria added. "Too bad we don't have flashlights."

"Be right back." Ruth lifted her index finger and then hustled down the hall and out of sight.

"Let me guess," Dot said as she watched her leave. "Ruth brought flashlights."

"I thought she packed a little heavy for seven nights," Margaret said.

Ruth returned moments later and handed Gloria and Margaret each a flashlight. "Sorry. I only brought three," she told the others.

The women headed to the stairs and made their way down to deck seven.

Gloria studied the passengers they passed by...happy, carefree and enjoying their vacation. She wondered if any of them had noticed the ship was no longer moving. Perhaps some of the more savvy passengers or those guests with military backgrounds had noticed.

"Here it is." Andrea stopped abruptly in front of a large, metal door with a round glass window. She peeked inside. "Who are we looking for?"

"Annette," Gloria and Lucy said in unison.

"Although I don't know what she looks like," Gloria admitted. She led the way as she eased the door open and the girls shuffled in single file.

The kitchen was massive with several long, stainless steel counters. There were tall cabinets lining the walls and off to one side was a large, stainless steel sink. Next to the sink was another, smaller room and she caught a glimpse of long shelves lined with canned goods.

"Hi. Can I help you?" A young girl with bright red hair and an anxious expression approached.

"We're looking for Annette," Liz said.

"Annette Delacroix?" the girl asked.

"I guess," Gloria said. "I'm Millie's cousin," she added, not sure if it would make one iota difference.

"Yes. Millie." The girl nodded. "Annette is around here somewhere. I'll be right back."

The girl wove her way around the counters. She passed by an entire counter covered in delicious desserts, including chocolate covered strawberries that made Gloria's mouth water and disappeared around the corner.

She returned moments later, followed by a woman with curly brown hair and an athletic build.

"Thank you Grace." The woman dismissed the young girl and turned her attention to Gloria and the gang. "I'm Annette Delacroix. How can I help you?"

The woman's piercing blue eyes didn't miss a thing as she studied the women in front of her, as if they were some sort of fascinating insect.

Gloria took a step forward. "I'm Gloria Kennedy, Millie's cousin. We wondered if we could talk to you for a moment."

Annette's expression softened. "Ah, the infamous Cousin Gloria whose exploits Millie greatly admires."

Gloria grinned. "I heard you two don't do too badly yourselves," she shot back.

Annette shrugged. "Yeah. We've had a few adventures. So what brings you to my neck of the woods?"

Liz stepped forward and lowered her voice. "Is there somewhere we can talk in private?"

"Follow me." Annette turned on her heel, headed to the other end of the kitchen and stopped in the far corner, away from the other workers. "What's up?"

Gloria briefly explained what had transpired and what Millie had told them, some of which she guessed Annette may have already known. When she got to the part where Gloria mentioned it was not Captain Armati's birthday, Annette held up a hand.

"Wait a minute!" She ran a hand through her curly dark hair and began pacing back and forth. "If what you're saying is true, Amit may have walked straight into a trap."

Annette stopped. "I've been wondering what happened to him. I sent him up to the bridge with the cake and he never came back."

"We can search for him," Frances offered.

"With eight of us, we should be able to find him," Dot added, and then immediately regretted offering since she knew Gloria was a magnet for trouble.

"If you don't mind," Annette said. "I can't leave the kitchen right now."

"How do we get to the bridge?" Lucy asked.

Annette opened the drawer of a nearby cabinet, pulled out a Siren of the Seas deck plan and unfolded it.

The girls crowded around as Annette explained the quickest way to reach the bridge. She handed the deck plan to Gloria. "I'll never forgive myself if something happens to Amit."

Dot touched Annette's arm. "We'll do our best to find Amit and no matter what, we'll come back to tell you what we did find."

"Thanks," Annette's lips curved in a half-hearted smile. "I would appreciate that." She followed them to the galley door and the women stepped out into the hall.

Gloria glanced back at the swinging door. "Let's get this search party underway."

***

Millie sucked in a deep breath and stepped out onto the stage. She had bigger fish to fry than to worry about a few hundred people staring at her while she fumbled through her opening lines.

The theater was packed, Millie's introduction went off without a hitch, and when she swept the curtain to the side to make her way backstage, she ran smack dab into Danielle.

Danielle grabbed Millie's arm and propelled her to the side. "What is going on?"

133

"What do you mean?" Millie asked.

"The ship isn't moving," Danielle hissed under her breath. "It's crawling with security. Not only that, I can't find Andy and you have suddenly become the Vanna White of cruise ship entertainment."

"Follow me." Millie, followed by Danielle, headed out of the theater, through the double doors and onto an open deck. "No one can reach the bridge or the engine room, the doors are locked and none of our access cards work."

"Someone has taken over the ship," Danielle eyes widened. "It all makes sense now. First, someone vandalizes Andy's cabin and then tries to break into Pursuer Donovan Sweeney's office. Someone was looking for something; an access card would be my guess."

Millie hadn't considered that angle, hadn't had time to consider that angle. "Annette mentioned earlier someone had ordered a birthday cake to be delivered to the bridge because it was Captain

Armati's birthday but Andy told me his birthday is Christmas Eve. It must have been a ploy to gain access to the bridge."

"Amit!" Millie's eyes widened in horror as it dawned on her what had happened. "Annette was going to send Amit to the bridge with the cake!"

"Which means Amit is in danger." Millie left Danielle near the rail and power walked across the deck toward the galley.

Danielle easily caught up. "Oh no, sister! We're in this together!" she vowed as she fell into step with Millie.

The women hustled to the galley and Millie flung open the door, her eyes scanning the room. She spotted Annette off in the corner, brandishing a meat tenderizer and pounding a piece of steak into submission.

"Amit!" Millie blurted out when she spotted her friend.

Annette glanced up, a spark of determination in her eyes. "Amit is missing. Your cousins and their friends are searching for him now."

Millie marched across the room. "What do you mean they're searching for Amit?"

Annette took one more whack at the steak and then set her weapon down. "They stopped by here earlier to tell me what was going on. I told them about the cake, how someone had ordered it for Captain Armati's birthday. Your cousin said it wasn't the captain's birthday. I sent Amit up to the bridge with the cake and he never came back."

Annette picked up the pointed tool and shook it in her hand. "I'm waiting for Sous-chef Marc Gravois to show up so I can join the search. I'm gonna find Amit if I have to tear this ship apart, bolt-by-bolt," Annette vowed.

Despite Annette's strong words, Millie spied a tiny crack in her friend's armor and a flicker of worry in her eyes. Annette and Amit were close...like mother and son.

"We'll wait with you and then search together," Millie promised her friend.

"Unless your cousins and their friends find him first," Annette said.

A burst of heat burned Millie's ears at Annette's words. This was Millie's stomping ground and her territory. Gloria and Liz should not be sticking their noses in where they didn't belong! Not only that, Millie knew the ship like the back of her hand. If anyone could find Amit, it was Millie!

Millie clenched her jaw and forced a smile. "I hope so, too." She did hope Amit was found safe and sound, but for heaven's sakes, did Gloria have to be the one to find him? Didn't the woman ever want to take a break from sleuthing?

The sous-chef arrived a short time later and assured Annette he would cover for her and to not worry about finishing her shift.

Millie, Annette and Danielle made their way into the hallway.

"Let's go find Amit," Millie said.

Chapter Ten

Gloria and the girls stared at the white metal door with the red and white sign that read, "Restricted Area. Authorized Personnel Only."

"Now what?" Ruth asked.

"We work our way backward," Gloria decided. "Assuming Amit made it this far." She took a step back. "Perhaps his attacker surprised him, came up behind him while he was waiting for someone to open the door to the bridge."

The girls retraced their steps, stopping at every door and peering inside.

The eight of them split up and scoured the area surrounding the bridge, returning a short time later without turning over a single clue.

"This was a complete waste of time," Liz griped. "We missed the first headliner show all because of some conspiracy theory." She glanced at her watch. "If I go now, I'll have just enough time to catch the second show."

"I-I'll go with you," Frances offered. She shrugged her shoulders at Gloria as if to say she was sorry, and then trailed behind Liz as they strolled to the bank of elevators.

The elevator doors opened. Liz turned her nose, tilted her chin and stepped inside.

"I hope she doesn't get stuck between floors," Gloria joked as she watched the doors close.

"Maybe we should go back to our balcony and keep an eye on the bridge," Lucy suggested.

"I guess." Gloria gazed one last time at the bridge door, wishing she had some way to sneak inside, before reluctantly following her friends down the stairs.

"I think I'll head down to the theater to watch the show," Margaret decided.

"Me too," Andrea said and then she looked at Gloria. "If you don't mind."

"Not at all. Be my guest. I'm not in the mood." Gloria turned to her friends. "Why don't you all go and enjoy the evening."

Lucy shook her head. "Nah. I'll hang out with you if you don't mind."

Andrea, Margaret, Dot and Ruth continued down the steps and headed to the theater.

Lucy and Gloria made their way to the galley to let Annette know they had come up empty-handed, but the man inside the kitchen told them she had left for the day so they headed back to the suite.

When they reached the suite, Gloria swiped her keycard and stepped inside. Lucy closed the door behind them before heading to the balcony.

Gloria dropped her keycard on the coffee table and followed her friend outside. "This ship is not moving. There's something going on. I can feel it in my bones."

"Maybe you should let Millie handle this one, after all this is her turf," Lucy wisely pointed out.

"True," Gloria admitted as she leaned her elbows on the railing and stared out at the dark waters. "Maybe I should butt out." She shifted her gaze to the bridge and a movement caught her eye.

"What did Ruth do with those binoculars?" she asked.

"They're on the coffee table." Lucy darted inside the suite and grabbed the binoculars. She stepped back out onto the balcony and placed them in Gloria's hand.

Gloria lifted the binoculars to her eyes, rolled the focus wheel and studied the dark waters. "Oh my gosh! Will you look at that!"

***

Millie stood in front of the door leading to the bridge and silently stared at it. "I could try my card again." She lifted the lanyard from around her neck and swiped her card through the slot. Nothing happened.

She grasped the door handle and quietly twisted. It wouldn't budge.

Millie stomped her foot, aggravated. "I wish I had x-ray vision and could see inside the bridge."

She leaned forward, placed her hands on her knees and tilted her head to the side as she studied the wall surrounding the door.

"Huh." She lifted her finger and swiped the wall. "Frosting," she announced as she held up her index finger.

Annette tipped her head and inspected Millie's finger. "Looks like the frosting that was on the captain's red velvet cake."

Annette ran her thumb across Millie's finger, removing a trace of the frosting and then licked her thumb. "Yep. That's it."

"Gross!" Danielle curled her lip.

Annette shifted her gaze and then rubbed the tip of her shoe across a faint white smear on the carpeted floor. "I have a theory. Follow along with me here...Amit made it this far with the cake. While he was waiting for someone to let him into the bridge, someone jumped him from behind, knocking the cake out of his hand."

"It's possible they overpowered Amit and now he's in the bridge, along with the captain and the others," Danielle added.

"True," Millie agreed. "But if you were attempting to hijack a ship, wouldn't you want as few captives as possible? Think about it. Power in numbers."

She lifted her slightly frosted finger. "One. Captain Armati." She lifted a second finger. "Two. Staff Captain Vitale. Then you have Ingrid and maybe even Amit. That makes at least four captives."

Annette clenched her jaw. "So you think they killed Amit and dumped his body overboard? If anything happens to Amit, I will never forgive myself."

"Which is why we have to keep moving, keep searching. There has to be something, some sort of clue," Millie said.

Danielle, Annette and Millie turned and slowly wandered down the hall. Lining the left hand side of the corridor were storage closets. As luck would have it, Millie had a master key to everything onboard the ship, including the storage closets.

She stopped in front of the first storage area, the one closest to the bridge, inserted her key and opened the door. The closet was full of cleaning supplies.

The closet next to it was chock full of bright orange life vests.

When Millie got to the third one, she paused. The cabinet was unlocked, the door slightly ajar. She stuck her finger on the edge of the frame and pulled.

The door swung open and a leg flopped out.

It was one of the maintenance crew...an unconscious maintenance crew; at least Millie prayed he was unconscious and not dead.

"Does he have a pulse?" Danielle bent down on one knee.

Annette dropped down next to Danielle, and pressed her index and middle finger to the side of his neck. "Yes!"

There was a large lump on his temple and his face was pale, but he was breathing. "Help me get him out," Annette said as she grabbed his arm and tugged.

Millie reached for his ankles while Annette grasped him under his arms.

"Hey!" Annette said. "Can you hear me?"

The man moaned.

The girls finally managed to drag him out of the closet and position him so that he was flat on his back.

Millie plucked her radio from her clip, turned it on and lifted it to her lips. "Doctor Gundervan, do you copy?"

"Go ahead Millie."

"We need you up on deck ten near the bridge. Stat."

"I'll be right there."

Millie leaned against the wall, keeping one eye on the hall and the other on the door to the bridge, half expecting a crazed killer to burst through the bridge door, guns blazing. "I really need to stop reading those scary books," she mumbled.

"Huh?" Annette lifted her head and gazed at her friend.

"Never mind," Millie said.

Thankfully, Doctor Gundervan appeared moments later. "Whatcha got, Millie?"

Gundervan shifted his gaze. "Oh no! What happened?" He dropped to his knees and set his black medical bag on the floor next to the unconscious man.

Annette crawled out of the way and the three women hovered nearby as they watched Doctor Gundervan examine the man.

While Doctor Gundervan checked his vitals, he began to come around. His eyes fluttered open and he stared blankly at Doctor Gundervan before shifting his gaze beyond the doctor. His eyes met Annette's. "Where am I?"

"I think he's going to be okay," Doctor Gundervan said. "Can you sit up?"

With the help of Doctor Gundervan, the man slowly eased to a sitting position. He gently placed his fingers against his swollen temple. "I don't know what happened. I was standing in the hall, looking at the surveillance camera. The next thing I know, my head hurts like the dickens and she is hovering over me." He pointed at Annette.

Gundervan eyed Annette and then shifted his gaze toward the bridge. "We should get him down to medical," he said.

The doctor helped the man to his feet and the two of them slowly shuffled down the hall to the bank of elevators.

Annette, Danielle and Millie trailed behind. They waited for Doctor Gundervan and the injured man to step into the elevator before following them in.

Millie clenched her teeth and nervously watched the elevator doors close, praying they wouldn't end up trapped inside.

When they reached the medical center, Annette, Danielle and Millie waited in the small reception area while Doctor Gundervan, accompanied by a nurse who met them at the door, helped the man into the back.

Annette paced the floor while Danielle and Millie watched the door to the examination room anxiously. "I wonder if he was able to catch a glimpse of his attacker."

Before Millie could reply, the door to the medical center burst open and Dave Patterson, accompanied by Purser Donovan Sweeney, stepped inside.

The sight of the two of them jogged Millie's memory. She popped out of the chair. "Oh my gosh! I'm supposed to open for the second seating show!"

Patterson waved his hand. "We just left Andy. He's on his way to the theater as we speak."

"Whew!" Millie wiped her brow. "I forgot all about it!"

Donovan nodded his head in the direction of the examination room. "What happened?"

Annette briefly explained how they had gone to the bridge and how Millie had found a small glob of frosting on the wall next to the door leading into the bridge.

"We started to search the storage closets near the bridge door and when we got to the third one, we found the maintenance guy unconscious and stuffed inside one of the closets," Millie explained.

Danielle crossed her arms and focused her razor sharp gaze on Dave Patterson. "Has someone hijacked Siren of the Seas?" she asked him point blank.

Patterson's eyes slid to Donovan Sweeney and then he gazed at Annette uneasily. "The short and sweet answer is yes. Someone has taken over both the bridge and the engine room. They have somehow managed to scramble all radio signals and communication. We're sitting ducks."

Donovan Sweeney quietly closed the outer door to the medical center and then shoved his hands in his front pockets. "We have several spotters patrolling the decks. It appears there is a boat out there lurking in the waters not far from Siren of the Seas."

Chapter Eleven

"Look at what?"

Gloria handed the binoculars to Lucy. "There is something out there in the water. See that small light?"

"Yeah. What do you think it is?" Lucy handed the binoculars back to Gloria.

"Hijackers...terrorists...accomplices of whoever has taken over this ship." The possibilities were endless – and frightening.

Gloria eased past Lucy and made her way into the suite. She grabbed the remote control and turned the television on. "Maybe there's something on the news," she said as she turned the volume up and flipped through the channels.

The only things showing were ship shows and a couple newly released movies. There were no weather channels, no national news. She shut the television off and dropped the remote on the bed. "That's odd."

"Do you think whomever took over the ship scrambled all the signals?" Lucy stepped over to the safe located inside the closet and swiped her card to unlock the thick metal door before reaching inside and pulling out her purse. "I'm going to check to see if my cell phone works."

It took several moments for the phone to power up and when it did, she turned it on, set it to roaming and studied the screen. Lucy shook her head. "I'm not getting a single bar. There's no signal."

A wave of fear washed over Gloria. The ship was not moving. The bridge and engine room were unresponsive and there was no way to contact anyone on shore. "This is much worse than I thought. I think a group of people have, for whatever reason, seized control of this ship."

The cabin door burst open and Dot, Margaret, Andrea and Ruth exploded into the room. "You missed a great show." Andrea vaulted onto the bed and placed her hands behind her head.

"Yeah. It was hilarious!" Liz agreed. "My stomach aches from laughing so hard."

"We stopped for a quick bite to eat and brought you back a snack." Dot was the last to enter the room. She slid two small plates of tempting treats on the desk. "One is bite size chicken lettuce wraps, and the other is shrimp and crab wonton."

"The sauce is to die for," Ruth told them.

"And we brought this back for you." Margaret unwrapped a paper napkin and handed Lucy a coconut macaroon dipped in dark chocolate.

Lucy grabbed the tasty treat and nibbled the edge. "Great. My last sweet treat before I'm killed," she joked.

Gloria lowered her gaze and gave her friend a warning look.

Andrea slid off the bed and headed to the balcony. "You guys still spying on the bridge?" She grabbed the binoculars Gloria had left on the small table and then lifted them to her eyes. "There's something out there in the water."

"Yep," Gloria agreed. "I think the ship has been hijacked and the smaller vessel has something to do with the hijackers."

"That's not funny," Liz huffed. "Trying to scare us half to death just because you can't take a simple vacation without having some major mystery to solve."

Gloria shrugged. "Suit yourself." She picked up the small dish containing the chicken lettuce wrap and settled into the corner of the sofa.

Dot crossed her arms and gazed out onto the balcony. "Do you think so?"

A knock on the door saved Gloria from having to defend her theory.

Frances darted over the door, opened it a crack and peeked out before opening it wide.

Millie, Annette and Danielle stepped into the room and Frances closed the door behind them. "Good. You're all here. We need some help."

Millie quickly brought them up to speed and confirmed Gloria's suspicion that some sort of vessel was hovering nearby.

"We should call for help," Margaret suggested.

"The phones don't work," Gloria and Millie answered in unison.

"We already tried," Lucy said.

Millie placed both hands behind her back and leaned against the wall. "The signals are blocked and we have no communication outside the ship."

Danielle slumped into the desk chair and ran her hand through her hair. "We found a maintenance man unconscious in one of the storage closets not far from the bridge. The only thing he can remember is discovering someone had cut the wires to the surveillance camera outside the bridge. Next thing he knew, we were pulling him from the closet."

Gloria eyed her cousin, Millie. "You weren't able to find Amit either?"

"No." Annette's shoulders drooped. "We noticed a dab of frosting on the wall next to the entrance to the bridge but there was no trace of Amit."

"Some of Siren of the Seas security, along with three of the temporary employees who have now come forward and admitted they are undercover FBI agents are going to lower one of the lifeboats into the water and then head back to the small island of Vieques to get help," Millie explained.

"All we're supposed to do is keep the passengers calm until help arrives," Annette finished.

"How long will it take for them to return with help?" Frances asked.

Millie did the mental calculations. "We left San Juan almost five hours ago. The lifeboat can move a lot faster than the cruise ship so shave off a couple hours ...maybe three hours to get to Puerto Rico. Once they get there they'll have to find help, formulate a rescue plan and then return to the ship." She shrugged. "Maybe twelve hours?"

Gloria frowned. They might not have twelve hours, depending on what the hijackers planned to do with the cruise ship and passengers, not to mention the crew.

"There's a mole," Millie said. "Someone who works on this ship is in on it. If we could figure out who that person is, we might be able to discover a gap in the hijackers plan and rescue the captain, crew and staff."

Gloria secretly wondered if this "Amit" was the mole. Based on Annette's reaction to her employee going missing, she wouldn't take kindly to that theory so Gloria kept the thought to herself.

Annette nodded. "If we had some way to set up a surveillance of the bridge and / or engine room, we might be able to get a hit on the perp."

"Wouldn't security be able to set up some sort of surveillance?" Ruth, the surveillance expert, asked.

"I asked the same question," Millie said, "and they basically told me to butt out, that they are working on it and to stay out of the way."

She went on. "We were told our job is to keep the guests calm and happy."

"I...might be able to help out," Ruth said casually as she inspected her fingernails. "Depending on the type...and amount of equipment you want."

She wandered over to the adjoining suite and returned moments later, dragging a large suitcase behind her. Ruth laid it on the floor, unzipped the cover and flung the top open.

The girls gathered around Ruth and peered into the open suitcase.

"Good grief, Ruth! What on earth?" Gloria sighed.

"I can tell you what it is." Annette reached inside, grabbed a pencil thin black stick and turned it over in her hand. "This is the Silo 450 zip camera with wide lens. I've been eyeballing one of these."

Ruth grinned. "Just got this baby last week. I ordered it from SpyCom in Virginia and since I ordered three, I got the third one half off." She plucked one from the suitcase and held it up. "See the little eye right there?"

Annette and Ruth began talking spy lingo, to which Gloria groaned and Millie rolled her eyes. "Oh no. Here we go."

Annette was like a kid in a candy store as Ruth unpacked her spy equipment and showed her everything she had brought onboard. She looked up, her eyes gleaming. "Man! I hope we get to use some of this cool stuff," she exclaimed.

"Until Dave Patterson and the agents discover we're working on our own recon," Danielle pointed out.

"We'll stay out of the way," Millie said.

Ruth carefully placed two of the Silo slim 450 zip cameras on the floor before packing the rest of her "essential" spy gear back inside the suitcase and zipping it shut. "I have more, but these two," she pointed at Millie and Gloria, "are chomping at the bit to set up surveillance."

"I'd love to help," Annette said eagerly.

"Have at it," Gloria said. "I'm willing to leave it to the so-called experts and just tag along."

Ruth led the way with Annette hot on her heels as the girls...all eleven of them headed out to set up surveillance.

Chapter Twelve

"I need a chair or a ladder...or even a pail to stand on." Ruth teetered on her tiptoes and attempted to mount the small camera in the corner of the hall.

"Shh." Gloria placed her index fingers to her lips and Millie pointed at the bridge door.

"Don't shush me," Ruth gasped. "I need help!"

Millie remembered seeing a mop bucket inside one of the closets earlier when they had searched for Amit. She opened the closet door, reached inside and pulled out the bucket before placing it upside down and sliding it to the corner for Ruth to stand on.

"Thanks." Ruth smiled at Millie and frowned at Gloria.

"This isn't my ship," Gloria pointed out.

Ruth got back to work as she carefully pressed the tiny spy camera in the upper corner of the hall. "Don't let me forget it."

Lucy snorted. "Like you'll ever leave a single piece of precious surveillance equipment behind."

"Let's move onto the engine room," Millie suggested, in an attempt to diffuse the tense situation between Ruth and Gloria, which was nothing, the banter between them more of teasing each other.

Millie led the way as they descended the stairs, going below the deck that contained the crew quarters. They were officially in the bowels of the ship.

Andrea shivered as she shifted her eyes and gazed overhead at the clanking pipes. "This place gives me the creeps."

"Me too," Danielle agreed. "I don't believe I've ever been down here before."

The path leading to the engine room was narrow and the girls had to walk single file. It was a good thing Millie knew where she was going because it was maze of twists and turns. They walked down a long hall and Millie turned right.

"You're going the wrong way. It's to the left," Annette said. "Follow me."

The women backtracked and followed Annette until she stopped abruptly in front of a round metal door with bold red letters, *Restricted Area,* emblazoned across the front. "This is it," she said in a low voice.

Ruth shifted her small satchel of surveillance equipment and carefully studied the hall. "This is perfect. There are a million places to hide a small piece of spy equipment."

She lowered her bag to the floor, unclasped the front and reached inside. Next to the door was a set of metal steps leading to nowhere. "This will work. Hold this."

She handed the small surveillance camera to Annette and climbed the ladder. When her head bumped the pipe above, she looked down. "Hand me the camera."

Annette handed her the small gadget and they all watched as Ruth carefully pressed the surveillance camera against a metal pipe directly overhead.

"Are you sure it will capture anyone going in or coming out of the engine room?" Margaret asked.

Ruth wiped the palms of her hands on the front of her slacks. "Guaranteed or your money back," she quipped as she backed down the ladder. "Now, all we have to do is sit back and watch."

"I'm hungry," Millie announced when they reached civilization aka the passenger area.

"Me too," Gloria said. "Dinner was an eternity ago."

"Margaret and I can pick up a few pizzas down at the pizza place and bring them back," Dot suggested.

The women parted ways when Margaret and Dot headed across the pool deck to the back of the ship where the fresh, made-to-order pizza station was located.

Gloria led the way back to the suites and as soon as they were inside, Ruth and Annette began setting up a temporary command center. The women settled in at the table in the corner while Gloria, Liz, Frances, Lucy and Millie headed to the balcony.

Danielle and Andrea plopped onto the small sofa to watch a rerun of the previous evening's show.

Millie rested her elbows on the railing and gazed wistfully at the bridge. "I wish I knew what was going on in there." Amit was missing. Captain Armati and Captain Vitale were being held against their will inside the bridge. Perhaps they were hurt or worse yet, dead.

She remembered watching from Liz's balcony as someone hit either Captain Armati or Captain Vitale on the back of the head and then dragged them from sight.

Millie looked straight down. A shadow from the slider directly below caught her eye. She gazed at the bridge again, and then shifted it to straight below.

Millie had been inside Captain Armati's apartment numerous times, not to mention out on his deck...that was directly below not only Gloria's suite but also her friend's suite!

"Oh my gosh!" Her mind began to race as she stuck her head into the room. "Does anyone have a selfie stick, one with an extension?"

Andrea lowered the volume on the television. "I have one. It's in my suitcase."

"I need to borrow it if you don't mind," Millie said. "I also need some duct tape."

Gloria followed Millie into the suite. She turned to Ruth. "You got any duct tape in that magic bag of tricks you brought?"

Ruth frowned. "No! I packed it but the darn roll was gonna push me over the baggage weight limit at the airport so I had to leave it at home. I thought about packing it in my carry-on bag but wasn't sure security would let me through with a roll of duct tape."

"I have a roll of duct tape," Liz said.

"Huh?" Gloria stared at her sister.

Liz shrugged. "What? Haven't you read any of those cruise trips books where they tell you to pack a roll of duct tape for emergencies? Why, that stuff can fix nearly anything."

"Can I borrow it?" Millie asked.

"Sure." Liz exited the cabin and returned moments later with a brand spanking new roll of silver duct tape. "Here you go." She handed it to Millie, who was already holding the selfie stick Andrea had given her.

"What's the plan?" Gloria watched as her cousin placed the selfie stick, roll of duct tape and her cell phone on the edge of the bed.

"There's a hall that connects the bridge to Captain Armati's apartment, which means his apartment is directly below your suite...and the one next door. I am going to put my phone on the end of the selfie stick, lower it down off the edge of the balcony and record some footage of the inside of the captain's apartment."

"If the curtains are open," Ruth pointed out.

"True." Millie nodded. "They should be. Captain Armati has a teacup Yorkie, Scout. Scout has a small grassy area at the end of the balcony, which is where the captain lets him out to take care of his business. The slider is open almost all the time." She placed her phone in the slot and then tightened the thumbscrew to secure it.

"What is the duct tape for?" Lucy asked.

"This is a little extra security in case the phone somehow manages to come loose. If it falls off, it's gonna be bye-bye phone," Millie said.

She peeled a piece of the sticky tape off the roll and tore the end before sticking one end on the edge of her phone and the other end on a small section of the black selfie stick. She firmly rubbed both ends of the tape. "That should do the trick."

Ruth stayed near her laptop to keep an eye on the surveillance cameras while the others followed Millie and her makeshift spy equipment out onto the balcony.

Millie turned her phone on and switched to recording mode before extending the selfie stick all the way out. "Here goes nothing."

Millie sucked in a breath and carefully lowered the stick - and her phone - over the side of the balcony.

She was careful not to lower it too far down, in case someone inside the apartment, namely the captors, happened to be looking out.

Millie waited a few seconds and then lifted the phone, turned the stick over and played back what the phone had recorded. The video was disappointingly dark.

"I can see a soft glow from below. Either it wasn't down far enough or the lights are off," Gloria said as she stared at the dark screen. "Try again."

Millie switched it to record again and lowered the phone even further. She slowly shuffled along the edge of the railing in an attempt to record several angles of the inside of the apartment directly below them.

She moved back and forth along the rail and then pulled the selfie stick and phone up. "Let's see what we've got."

Dot and Margaret arrived moments later carrying three pizza boxes, several cans of Diet

Coke and regular Coke, along with plates, plastic cups and silverware. "Piping hot pizza, right out of the oven!" Dot declared.

Although Millie was dying to see what they had caught on tape, she didn't want the food to get cold. "We can eat first, and then check out the video," she suggested.

They all loaded their plates with pizza and sat on the chairs, the couch, the edge of the bed and even the balcony furniture.

"The only one missing is Cat," Millie commented to Annette.

"She's had enough on her plate lately," Danielle said.

It was true. Cat had been through a lot, which reminded Millie that Cat needed help. As soon as the current crisis was over, she vowed to focus on helping Cat.

"We should pray," Gloria said.

All of the women bowed their heads. "Dear Lord, we thank you for this food and pray you bless it to our bodies. We pray for poor Amit, for Captain Armati and the others in the bridge and in the engine room, that you protect them. We also pray for a swift and successful rescue mission with no injury or loss of life. Thank you Lord."

The prayer ended with an echo of "amens."

Millie quickly finished her pizza, wiped her mouth with the napkin and placed the napkin on top of her plate. She was anxious to see if the phone had recorded anything that might be useful.

Gloria, who was on the same wavelength, quickly finished her food. She settled in next to Millie as her cousin removed the phone and tape from the selfie stick and placed the stick on the bed. She turned the phone over.

The other girls huddled around, everyone except for Ruth, whose eyes never left the computer screen, and Margaret and Dot, who had no idea what the others were looking at.

At first, there was nothing on the screen but as the phone moved along the rail, the screen grew brighter and finally, they were able to see inside Captain Armati's apartment.

Millie didn't recognize two of the men who walked by the open slider, but she did recognize the third person...it was Purser Donovan Sweeney!

Chapter Thirteen

"What in the world?" Millie blurted out.

"That's Donovan Sweeney," Danielle gasped.

"You're kidding!" Annette peered over Millie's shoulder.

"Who is Donovan Sweeney?" Lucy asked.

"Purser Donovan Sweeney. Donovan is like the ship's banker," Millie explained. "He controls all the money onboard the ship, along with handling crew tips, salary and new hires."

Millie pressed the button on the phone to replay the recording. She leaned in to study it carefully.

Donovan walked by the phone once, and then a second time. She studied his expression. He didn't appear to be under duress. In fact, he looked calm, although Millie had never seen Donovan Sweeney anything but calm. "I don't know what to make of it," she admitted.

Donovan was the only person Millie recognized. She had been hoping to catch a glimpse of Captain Armati and Staff Captain Vitale, to have some sort of reassurance they were unharmed.

"Did you see Amit?" Annette asked.

"No," Millie shook her head. "We can try again." She secured the phone to the selfie stick, affixed a new piece of duct tape to both the phone and selfie stick and walked back out onto the balcony where she lowered the phone over the side again. She tried twice and both times, the screen was dark.

Millie turned her head and glanced at Danielle who was hovering in the doorway. "Close the door and pull the curtains so it's dark out here."

Danielle nodded and quickly slid the door shut and then closed the curtains.

Millie, along with Gloria, Lucy, Andrea and Liz leaned over the side and looked down. There was no longer a dim light coming from the apartment below.

"They shut the curtains," Gloria said.

"Might as well call it a night," Andrea said as she lifted her arms above her head and stretched her back. "I'm whupped."

"Me too," Lucy agreed.

The women headed back inside and Gloria quietly closed the slider, clicked the lock and tugged the edge of the curtains.

Millie carefully removed the piece of duct tape, loosened the screws on the selfie stick and then handed it to Andrea. "Thanks for the loan. I should head out to check on Andy."

Annette nodded. "I need to check on the galley and make sure my replacement didn't screw everything up."

Gloria walked them to the door and waited for them to step into the hall. "We'll keep you posted if we see anything on Ruth's surveillance cameras," she promised.

Danielle headed to the cabin, Annette to the galley and Millie headed to Andy's office to fill him in.

She found him hunched over his desk as he studied his daily planner. He looked up when he heard Millie's footsteps. "There you are," he said as he pulled off his reading glasses. "I was just about to send out a search party. You were MIA for the second show."

"Sorry. I got sidetracked." Millie eased into the seat next to Andy and leaned back in the chair as she rubbed her brow. "I heard some of the crew took one of the lifeboats and are on their way back to Puerto Rico to get help."

"Yeah, that's what Patterson and the others have been working on. Majestic Cruise Lines is aware of the situation so I'm sure authorities are aware as well."

Millie snapped to attention. "How...do you know?"

"Dave Patterson and the undercover agents were able to briefly get through to the mainland. The hijackers are demanding fifty million dollars in exchange for the safe release of the captain, crew and ship. They gave the cruise line until six o'clock tomorrow night to drop a bag with the unmarked bills on the helipad or they're going to start killing crew and then passengers every hour on the hour."

He went on. "Donovan Sweeney offered to try to negotiate with the captors but I don't know what happened." Andy smiled grimly. "I had to get back here. The show must go on."

Had Donovan Sweeney somehow managed to make it inside the bridge and was now being held captive as well? Wouldn't he be a prize prisoner...the purser of the ship?

Millie's mind was spinning. Perhaps it was something much more sinister and Donovan

Sweeney was in on it. He had certainly appeared calm, cool and collected on video as he casually strolled around Captain Armati's apartment.

"I saw Donovan Sweeney a short time ago, walking around Captain Armati's apartment," Millie said.

Andy jerked forward. "You did? How did you…"

"If you remember, my cousin, Gloria, her suite is one deck up from the outboard bridge wing which means her suite is also directly above Captain Armati's apartment so I got the bright idea to hook my phone to a selfie stick. I lowered it over the side of her balcony to try to capture some footage of the inside of the captain's apartment."

She pulled the phone from her front pocket, switched it on and then hit play for the video footage before handing it to Andy. "Check it out."

Andy studied the footage. "I-I...we need to get this to Dave Patterson." He shoved his chair back, knocking it over in his haste.

They walked silently out of Andy's office, across the stage and out of the theater. The halls were quiet. Most passengers either had turned in for the night or were enjoying some late night entertainment in one of the bars, nightclubs or the ship's casino.

There were a few stragglers wandering around and Millie smiled as she passed them. She wondered how many of them had noticed the ship was not moving. Surely, some of the more seasoned cruisers would have noticed.

"Have any of the passengers asked why the ship isn't moving?" Millie whispered as they walked.

"A couple," Andy admitted. "I've blown it off and told them we were ahead of schedule and the captain was running some evening safety exercises in the open water."

The lights in the security office were on. Andy lightly tapped on the door, turned the knob and opened the door.

Dave Patterson was sitting behind his desk. He waved them in. "Come on in. You know the saying, misery loves company."

Patterson swiveled in his chair and gazed at Millie, a haggard expression on his face. "The crew attempted to abort the trip to Puerto Rico."

Dave Patterson ran a hand through his hair. "The hijackers must have seen them as they attempted to return to the ship. According to one of my men who was on the sky deck, trying to help them make it back, someone from near the panorama deck fired off some shots so the boat took off. Hopefully everyone is okay and they can make it to shore."

Millie's mouth dropped open and she blinked rapidly as she tried to absorb what Patterson had said. "Not only are they hijackers, they're attempted murderers."

Andy placed Millie's phone on the desk. "You can't blame yourself, Dave. You did what was best, what you needed to do."

"Hopefully they're alright," Millie said.

Patterson nodded. "They were still a ways out from the ship so I'm praying they're all okay. There's no video footage since it was too dark to pick anything up on the exterior surveillance cameras."

"Speaking of footage, Millie was able to get some footage of the inside of Captain Armati's apartment. You'll want to see this."

Dave Patterson reached for the phone, flipped it over and turned it on. His eyes narrowed as he silently watched the video. "Donovan went to the bridge earlier to try to negotiate with the hijackers."

Patterson turned the phone off, leaned forward and slid it across the desk. "How did you get this? Rappel down the side of the cruise ship and hang off the side while holding your phone?"

Millie shook her head. "No. It was easier than that. The suite my cousin, Gloria, is staying in is directly above Captain Armati's apartment. I attached my phone to a selfie stick and lowered it over the side of the balcony."

Patterson drummed the tips of his fingers on the top of the desk thoughtfully. "Their balcony may be our way in. I never thought of it. We've been trying to gain access to the engine room, but maybe we need to start with the bridge first."

He stood. "I have a skeleton security crew along with several of the FBI agents who have come forward. They're patrolling the ship and are on standby. There's not much we can do tonight and my brain is fried from trying to find a way out of this mess. I think I'll try to get a couple hours sleep."

Dave Patterson pointed to a small, narrow cot in the corner of his office, something Millie hadn't noticed earlier. "Tomorrow is going to be a long day."

Andy and Millie made their way out of Patterson's office and down the long, empty hall to the stairs. They descended the steps and parted way on "I-95," the nickname the crew had long ago given the crew hallway, which ran the entire length of the ship.

"I'll see you first thing in the morning," Andy said. He turned to go and then turned back. "Try to stay out of trouble tonight," he said.

Millie yawned and then covered her mouth. "I'm too tired to get into trouble." Her steps dragged as she walked down the empty hall to the cabin she shared with Danielle.

The cabin was dark so she quietly closed the door behind her.

Millie tiptoed to the bathroom, peeled her clothes off and slipped into her pajamas before brushing her teeth, splashing cold water on her face and heading to bed.

The hum of the forced air through the ac vents filled the air, along with Danielle's soft snores.

Millie lifted the covers and slipped between the cool sheets.

She clasped her hands and began to pray. "Dear God, please help Dave Patterson and his crew rescue our ship. I pray for the men who were in the rescue boat, that they safely make it to shore. Please protect my family, too. In Jesus' name, amen."

Millie's hands dropped to her sides and she was out like a light.

***

Danielle shaded her eyes and gazed out at the serene waters of Lake Mirror. The backdrop of the mountains glimmered across the deep blue waters of the lake. It reminded Danielle of a painting and she sucked in a deep breath, soaking it all in.

"Hey knucklehead! I thought you were picking wild berries for the pie you promised to make me!"

Danielle spun around and beamed at the handsome young man who had come up behind her. He playfully punched Danielle in the arm, his mischievous eyes dancing.

"I was on my way," she said as she nodded at the small fishing boat, propped up against a boulder and half hidden by thick, tall grass. "Maybe after I finish picking berries, we can go fishing," she said hopefully.

"Right after you make my pie." He reached up and wiped the droplets of sweat from his brow. "Whew! This day is gonna be a scorcher and the lake looks mighty tempting."

"Race you to the water!" He didn't wait for a reply and quickly took off.

"Casey! That's not fair!" Danielle sprinted across the field of wildflowers in hot pursuit of her brother, but Casey easily reached the water's edge first.

He knelt down and sifted through the smooth stones surrounding the lake until he found the perfect one. He picked the stone up and studied it as he ran his thumb over the smooth surface.

"Check this out." Casey flicked his wrist and sent the stone skimming across the tranquil waters.

"You still haven't taught me how to do that," Danielle scolded when she got close.

Casey tilted his head and grinned. "Because you're a slow learner," he teased and then bent down to find another stone. He picked it up, turned it over and nodded. "This'll do. Now watch."

He demonstrated his stone skimming technique and anxious to try it, Danielle began sifting through the stones, searching for the perfect one.

She kicked the stones with the tip of her foot and spied one that looked promising. Danielle bent down and picked it up.

Casey gazed at the rock in her hand. "Not that one!" He pointed at the stone. "Look. This one is special. This side is the color of your eyes." He flipped it over in her hand. "And this side is the color of my eyes. See?"

He was right. Each side of the rock was a different shade – one side a lighter blue and the other side a deeper blue. She rubbed her thumb over the lighter side, the one that was more her shade.

"You have to keep this rock. It will bring you luck. Plus, whenever you look at it, it will remind you of me!" he told her.

"You're right." Danielle nodded as she rubbed the small stone thoughtfully. "I'll keep it forever." She slipped it in her pocket and reached for another one.

"I have a surprise for you," Casey told her before he spun around and jogged around the edge of the lake. "I'll be right back."

Danielle's heart began to race and a wave of fear washed over her. Warning bells went off in her head and her blood ran cold. Something bad was about to happen.

"Wait!" She reached out to grab Casey's arm. "Don't go!" She tried desperately to grab his arm, to stop him, but she was clutching thin air.

Casey had already circled around the edge of the lake as he headed toward the cabin on the other side.

Danielle chased after him, but it was too late. She watched in horror as her beloved brother abruptly stopped in his tracks. He swayed for a moment and then his body crumpled to the ground.

"No! Casey!" Danielle raced along the water, her entire body, her mind focused on reaching her brother. It was as if she was moving in slow motion. The faster she ran, the slower she moved.

When she finally reached Casey, he was lying on the ground, face down.

Danielle dropped to her knees. "No!" she cried in anguish as she rolled her brother over and cradled him in her arms.

His eyes were closed, his body lifeless. A small trickle of blood ran down his temple. "No!"

***

"*No...no...*"

"*ahh...ahh...NO!*"

Millie's eyes flew open.

Something had awoken her and then she realized it was a sound and the sound was coming from the bunk above hers.

"*ahhhh!*"

Millie sat up in bed. "Danielle?"

Gasp.

Millie flung back her covers. Something was wrong with Danielle!

She quickly switched on the small nightlight next to her bed. Millie hadn't quite managed to clear the bed and whacked the back of her head on the edge as she tried to stand.

"Ouch!" She held the back of her head and gazed into the top bunk.

Danielle was sitting upright, staring straight ahead, a blank expression on her face.

Millie gently touched her arm. "Danielle. Are you okay?"

Danielle jerked her head and looked at Millie, a flicker of recognition in her eyes. Her shoulders slumped. "I...I was having a bad dream."

She flopped back down in her bunk, pulled the covers to her chin and squeezed her eyes shut.

Millie knew whatever Danielle had been dreaming about was still hovering on the edge of her mind. The young woman began to tremble violently and Millie's heart went out to her.

She slowly began rubbing the side of Danielle's arm, just as she had done for her own children years ago when they woke her in the middle of the night after having a bad dream.

Danielle started to relax. "I...thank you. I'm feeling better now."

Millie stayed for a few more moments and then patted the young woman's arm. "I'm here if you need me, dear," she said before crawling back into her bunk and shutting off the light.

Millie lay awake for a long time. This wasn't the first time Danielle had had nightmares. In fact, she had had several that had awoken both of them in the dead of the night.

They were always the same where Danielle woke up screaming "No" over and over, except this time, Millie could've sworn she had heard a name...Casey.

Not tonight, but soon, Millie would try to talk to the young girl who was obviously distraught over this "Casey."

She closed her eyes, prayed a heartfelt prayer for the young woman in the bunk above her and finally, Millie drifted off to sleep.

***

"What are you doing?" Gloria stepped into Margaret, Dot and Ruth's suite early the next morning and focused her eyes on Ruth, who sat in front of her computer staring at the screen.

Ruth gave Gloria a quick glance. "Keeping watch. I figured I would take the graveyard shift and then someone else could take over so I can get some rest."

"You mean you haven't slept at all?"

"Nope." Ruth shook her head. "Someone has to keep watch."

Margaret emerged from the bathroom. "Did Inspector Gadget tell you she has been up all night, staring at the computer screen and drinking Red Bull?"

Gloria wasn't surprised. She remembered the time Ruth had been under investigation at the post office and had stayed at Gloria's farm, monitoring the post office...day and night. "No." She slid the empty chair close to Ruth. "I can take over now," she offered.

"Thanks." Ruth eased out of the chair and groaned as she placed both hands on her back and stretched. "I'm getting too old for these marathon surveillance sessions." She shifted the laptop so it faced Gloria.

"Did you see anything?" Gloria asked.

"Yeah. A lot of security walking around and some of them even stopped, but no one came out or went in either the bridge or the engine room."

Ruth shuffled to the bathroom and Margaret waited until the door had closed. "The woman is obsessed with surveillance. I watched her until I finally fell asleep. I don't think she even bothered to blink."

"Yep. Sounds about right." Gloria nodded and then glanced at the empty beds. "What did you do with Dot?"

"She's out on the balcony drinking coffee," Margaret said. "We're waiting on room service. I had no idea we could order omelets, bacon, waffles...all sorts of goodies – and it's free!"

"Maybe we should try it." Andrea stepped into the room and caught the tail end of the conversation. "I found a room service menu and order sheet in one of our dresser drawers."

Gloria's stomach grumbled. The pizza they had indulged in the evening before was long gone. "Sounds good." She had better eat if she planned to be stuck in the room working a surveillance shift.

Andrea returned moments later, menu in hand.

Gloria selected an egg white omelet with ham, mushrooms, onions and light on the cheese along with a side of bacon and wheat toast. She handed the menu to Andrea. "Oh! Add coffee. Don't forget coffee."

Andrea nodded. "Right-o. I'll be back in a jiffy."

Lucy passed Andrea in the doorway, quickly placed her order and stepped into the room. "How did you all sleep?"

Dot opened the slider door. "I slept great. Ruth didn't sleep at all. She stayed up all night watching the stinkin' computer screen."

Ruth stepped out of the bathroom, clad in one of the crisp white bathrobes she had found in the closet, her hair wrapped in a turban. "Someone needs to take this crisis seriously. If this ship has been hijacked, we're all in danger."

It was true. Gloria shifted her gaze and stared out the slider at the calm seas. She wondered how Millie had survived the previous evening and if she had news on Amit, the bridge or the engine room.

Gloria had tried her cell phone as soon as she crawled out of bed. She had been anxious to talk to Paul, to see if he missed her as much as she missed him.

The suite door, which Andrea had left ajar, waiting for room service to deliver their breakfast, flew open and Liz burst into the room. "Someone just went overboard!"

The girls rushed out of the room, across the hall and onto the balcony where Frances stood, staring down. "Look. It's a woman and she's over there!"

Gloria leaned over the rail and studied the water. "We need Ruth's binoculars."

"Here!" Ruth still dressed in the robe, handed the binoculars to Gloria.

Gloria lifted them to her eyes and adjusted the dial as she gazed out into the water. The woman, her arms flailing wildly, bobbed up and down as she attempted to say afloat.

"I hope she knows how to swim," Lucy said.

Someone tossed a life preserver over the side of the ship and the woman began to tread water as she swam toward the orange vest.

The echo of voices filled the air as passengers and crew realized someone had gone overboard and attempted to help.

Gloria handed the binoculars to Ruth. "It looks like a ship employee, a woman. If I didn't know better, I would say it was that young blonde...Danica...Denise..."

"Danielle?" Andrea gasped. "Let me see!"

Chapter Fourteen

Andrea yanked the binoculars out of Ruth's hands and put them to her eyes. "Yeah! You're right. I bet fifty bucks that's her!"

Gloria cupped her hands to her mouth. "Danielle!"

They all held their breath as Danielle slipped the life vest over her head and shifted onto her back in an attempt to secure the front.

"And...it's on. She's on the move!" Liz reported. The girls cheered for Danielle.

Pop! Pop, pop! A quick succession of popping sounds filled the air.

Danielle ducked her head and began treading water in an attempt to reach the side of the ship and safety.

They heard it again.

Pop!

"That's the sound of gunfire!" Lucy yelled. "Someone is shooting at Danielle!"

The girls watched in horror as Danielle desperately tried to reach the side of the ship and safety.

People from all over, balconies next door and both above and below them began shouting.

"Go Danielle! Swim!" Gloria urged the girl. "You can do it!"

A bright orange life ring landed in the water, right next to Danielle. She plunged forward and wrapped her arms around the ring, which was attached to a rope.

She held it in a death grip and the ring quickly disappeared from sight. "I think she made it." Gloria shifted her gaze. The gunfire was coming from the front of the ship...and the bridge.

"The hijackers must have someone patrolling the front of the ship," Margaret said.

"Room service!" A uniformed crewmember peeked in the open door. He was holding two full room service trays. Right behind him was another crewmember, carrying an equally full tray of food. "Did someone order room service?"

"Yes. For both suites!" Gloria led one of them into their suite while Margaret led the other into theirs.

"You can put the trays here." Gloria pointed to the small table off to one side.

The crewmember placed the heavy trays on the table, and then transferred the plates from the tray to the table.

After all of the covered dishes were on the table, he removed the lids, shifted them to the center of the table and stood back waiting for the seal of approval.

"Perfect." Gloria nodded. "Thank you."

"We need to tip him," Andrea whispered. "I'll get it."

Andrea headed to the closet, opened the safe, pulled out her purse and wallet and returned with ten dollars. "Thank you so much."

The man grinned as he took the money. "Thank you. I come back tomorrow if you want," he said.

Gloria, Lucy and Andrea waited until he left and then closed the door behind him before settling in at the table.

The other girls, Margaret, Dot and Ruth gathered in the room next door and settled in to eat their breakfast as they discussed what had transpired.

"Wait for us!" Gloria hollered through the open door as she unwrapped her silverware and placed the cloth napkin in her lap.

The girls bowed their heads and prayed. "Thank you for this food, Lord. We pray for not only our safety but also the safety of the passengers and crew. Thank you."

"We also pray for the person who went overboard...the one we think may have been Danielle," Andrea added.

"Amen," Lucy finished.

Gloria shifted her omelet to make room for a slice of wheat toast. She eyed Lucy's breakfast plate, which consisted of chocolate chip pancakes, an order of sausage links and an array of glazed donuts.

She watched as her friend poured a generous amount of syrup on top of the pancakes and sawed off a thick chunk before popping it into her mouth. She propped her fork on the edge of her plate and chewed while Gloria grinned.

Lucy covered her mouth. "What?" she mumbled.

"You. That's all Lucy. Just watching you."

Andrea tore a chunk of white toast and dipped it in the center of her over-easy egg yolks.

"Makes you wonder how she can eat all sorts of sweet stuff and still stay so skinny."

Gloria had wondered the same thing for years, but Lucy seemed healthy and in shape so it wasn't Gloria's place to pass judgment, although personally, there was no way she could stomach all those sweets.

Ruth popped her head in the doorway. "Liz graciously offered to let me sleep in her suite where it's nice and quiet. Dot is watching the monitor. I'll see you later." She waved good-bye and headed out the door.

The rest of the posse, minus Dot, who had strict instructions from Ruth not to take her eyes off the screen, shuffled into the room. "What's the plan?" Margaret asked.

"My plan is to get some sun by the pool," Liz said. "We should let authorities handle the crisis situation. Plus, if we stick our noses in where they don't belong, we might end up getting shot at, too."

Gloria chewed on her piece of bacon. True. It was apparent whomever had taken control of the ship meant business. She was in unfamiliar territory. Maybe it was time to take a step back and assess the situation.

In the meantime, the girls could continue to monitor the cameras and perhaps attempt to record the captain's suite below. Maybe that would be their contribution.

"I wouldn't mind getting a little sun myself," Andrea admitted. "It seems a shame to miss out on all this beautiful weather and a chance to chillax."

"You all go on ahead to the pool. I'm going to track down Millie and make sure Danielle, if that was Danielle, is okay," Gloria told them.

They finished eating their breakfast, and then stacked their empty plates, cups and covers on the tray along with their dirty silverware before changing into pool attire and heading out.

Gloria waited until they were all gone. The only one left was Dot, who was still manning the computer monitor. "Why don't you head to the lido deck to enjoy the weather, too? I can watch the monitor," she told her friend.

"Nah!" Dot leaned back and gazed at Gloria. "I never was one for crowds and heat. I'm happy to hang out here."

She reached beside her, grabbed her e-reader and tapped the top. "Don't tell Ruth, but I have a new cozy mystery I started the other day and I might try to get a little reading in while everyone is gone."

Gloria pinched her fingers together and made a zipping motion across her lips. "My lips are sealed. I think I'll try to track down Millie to see if she has heard anything else."

She stepped back into her suite, grabbed her room card and shoved it into her pocket before heading out.

Gloria had no idea where to begin to look for Millie so she headed to guest services. Maybe they could help track her cousin down.

The line for the guest services stretched across the atrium, snaked around the side and into the hall. Gloria took one look at the long line and changed her mind. It would take hours to make it to the front of the line.

She remembered Millie mentioning she had to report to Andy's office, which was in the theater and located somewhere behind the stage.

Gloria grabbed a deck plan from the edge of the empty excursions counter and flipped it open. It wasn't far from where she was...only two decks down and in the back.

She headed to the elevators and then changed her mind, opting for the stairs and the exercise instead.

"O sixty-six."

"B twelve."

Gloria wandered into the theater and made her way down the center aisle. She gazed at the stage and spotted Millie, who was calling bingo.

Gloria eased into a cushioned theater seat to wait.

Millie caught her cousin's eye and winked. When the first game finished, Millie announced there would be a second game.

Gloria headed to the front to purchase a bingo card, figuring that if she had to wait, at least she could play. The game went quickly and Gloria was one call away from winning when someone else called bingo.

The game ended and passengers exited the theater while Gloria made her way to the front. She waited quietly while Millie and another crewmember put the bingo cards and wheel in the cabinet and then wheeled the cabinet off the stage.

Millie's head popped out from the side and she waved her cousin to the back. "We can talk in here."

Gloria followed Millie to the other side of the stage, down a short hall and into a brightly lit area.

The area boasted walls, but the walls didn't go all the way to the ceiling. She gazed up at the web of pipes and wires overhead. Off to one side was a narrow ladder that led to a catwalk. "This place must be creepy late at night."

Visions of shadowy figures popping out of dark corners filled Gloria's mind.

"It is," Millie said as she led her to the far corner.

She pulled out a chair for Gloria and then settled into the one next to it.

"How is Danielle?" Gloria asked.

"How did you..."

"Know? Because we had a bird's-eye view of the entire incident from Liz's balcony. What happened?"

Millie explained that Danielle, a tad on the impulsive side, decided to take matters into her own hands and scaled the side of the ship in an attempt to gain access to the bridge.

One of the hijackers spotted Danielle. When he got close, he began waving his gun at her.

Danielle tried to escape, lost her grip and fell into the water.

"Thankfully, one of the crew spotted her and threw her a lifejacket. Someone else tossed in a life ring, but not before one of the hijackers on lookout fired a couple shots at her in the water," Millie said.

"They missed?"

"Yep." Millie nodded. "Before she was spotted, she was able to catch a brief glimpse inside the bridge. She said she saw Captain

Armati, Staff Captain Vitale and the woman who runs the computers, Ingrid Kozlov. She also saw Amit, Annette's guy, along with Purser Donovan Sweeney."

"You're kidding," Gloria said. "At least they're all alive."

"There was one more," Millie said. "Dave Patterson, our head of security."

Chapter Fifteen

Gloria frowned. "What does that mean?"

"My guess is the hijackers are capturing our highest ranking officers one by one to add pressure to the cruise lines to cave to their demands."

Millie abruptly stood and began pacing the floor. "One of them is the mole. I feel it in my bones. The hijackers are demanding fifty million dollars be dropped off on the helipad by six o'clock tonight or they start killing crew and passengers and are going to toss their bodies over the side of the ship."

Millie paused. "Someone high up had to get the hijackers...and their weapons onboard. Security is tight, but if you knew the ins and outs of the ship and had high security clearance, it could be done."

"But how will they get off even if they do get the ransom money?" Gloria asked.

"There's some sort of ship not far from Siren of the Seas. I noticed it last night and I noticed it again this morning. It's possible they followed us from the Port of San Juan."

She went on. "Think about it. With millions of dollars, a yacht or smaller ship at your disposal, which just so happens to be sitting in international waters, the various countries could spend months arguing over whose responsibility it was. Meanwhile, the criminals are long gone, living the high life in some faraway country."

"But surely the cruise ship line would want their money back," Gloria pointed out.

"They don't have the manpower to search every country," Millie said. "Danielle kind of gave me an idea I'm tossing around."

She outlined her brief strategy to Gloria and Gloria added her own two cents. "First, we need to flush out the mole before the plan is implemented. Otherwise, rescuers may be walking right into a trap."

"True," Millie agreed. "What little Danielle was able to see, she wasn't able to gauge body language or any kind of clue as to who it might be. There were at least three other, unknown men inside the bridge."

"Millie? Are you back here?" Andy's booming voice echoed in the empty theater. He appeared moments later, followed by Oscar, Dave Patterson's second in command. There was another man too, the man Nikki had noticed hanging around the guest services.

Andy nodded at Gloria and turned his attention to Millie. "I've put Danielle on restriction. Any more antics like that and she could get our crew killed, not to mention herself!"

"At least she was able to see Patterson, Captain Armati, Captain Vitale and Donovan are all still alive." Millie leaned her elbows on the table. "Have we heard anything else on the ransom demands being met? We're running out of time."

Andy rubbed the day-old stubble on his chin. "No and the natives are getting restless. I just left guest services and the place is a madhouse. The passengers are irate because they can't use their phones. They know something is up because the ship isn't moving. We can't hold them off much longer without telling them something."

Gloria had a sudden thought. "What about lowering the lifeboats and getting people off the ship?"

"Already thought about that," Andy said. "We're afraid if we do, the hijackers will do the same thing they did to the crew last night when they attempted to get help."

"They fired shots at the lifeboat," Millie explained. "The crew was able to escape and we're holding out hope they made it to San Juan."

"Frank Bauer is on his way down here now. Maybe he can find a way into the bridge or engine room that no one else knows about," Andy said.

"Frank is head of maintenance," Millie told Gloria.

The agents, security and the others tossed out different ideas on how to gain access to the engine room and bridge but all the ideas had holes and they decided it would only put the crews' lives in even more danger.

Millie and Gloria sat quietly, hoping the others wouldn't notice them or ask them to leave.

A tall, balding man wearing a brown work outfit and carrying a long round paper tube appeared from the edge of the stage.

Annette Delacroix followed behind.

"Thanks for joining us, Frank," Andy said. "You too, Annette."

All eyes turned to Frank, their last hope.

Andy spoke. "Is there any way to penetrate the engine room or bridge? Perhaps a duct, vent or some sort of access panel?"

"Maybe." Frank pried the cover off the end of the tube, reached inside and pulled out a roll of papers – detailed blueprints of the ship's decks. He spread the large sheets out and Andy placed a stapler on one end, a tape dispenser catty corner and then held the other ends.

They all leaned forward to study the blueprints. "This is the engine room." Frank pointed to a section of the print.

He ran his index finger along the top. "There's a small vent leading to the engine room and on the other side of the vent is a catwalk. Well, maybe not even a catwalk but more like a metal runner that connects one end of the engine room to the other."

Andy interrupted. "Is it large enough for someone to crawl through the vent and gain access?"

Frank tapped his finger on top of the print. "It's possible, but they would have to be pretty small and spry. I don't think I could fit." He turned his gaze to Annette. "What do you think?"

Annette shifted to the side and studied the print. "I might be able to navigate through the pipe. Is there any way to take a look at it first?"

Frank nodded. "Of course. We can go now."

"No time like the present." Annette shifted the chair back and stood.

Oscar scrambled to his feet. He patted Annette on the back. "This is gonna remind you of the good ole days."

Annette shot him a dark look before shifting her gaze to Andy.

Millie tilted her head. She had always been suspicious her friend, Annette, had a story to tell, that there was more to her past than just being in the food and beverage business.

"The good ole days," Millie remarked. "I would *love* to hear about the good ole days, Annette. I'm sure it had something to do with rappelling down the side of cliffs, installing surveillance equipment in ductwork and hooking recording devices to the bottom of room service dishes."

Gloria grinned. "Sounds like some of my friends."

The stranger turned to Oscar as he rose to his feet. "The women must go. This doesn't concern them."

Millie opened her mouth to speak and then promptly closed it.

Gloria tugged on her cousin's arm. "Let's go."

Millie stomped across the stage and Gloria hurried behind her.

After the women left, the group made their way to the other end of the ship, passing by the chaos surrounding guest services.

"We have to do something about that," Andy said. "Hold up."

He made his way over to Nikki Tan, who looked as if she was about to burst into tears at any moment. Andy leaned forward and whispered in her ear.

Nikki swiped at her eyes and nodded.

"Poor thing," Annette said when Andy returned.

"I told her we would make an announcement over the intercom soon to address the guests' concerns."

"What are you going to say?" Frank asked.

"I don't know yet," Andy admitted. "I'm still working on it."

When they reached the stairs near the rear of the ship, or aft, they descended the stairs to the lowest deck before heading down a small hall.

Frank opened a metal door that read, "Authorized Personnel Only." He held it open while the others crossed the threshold.

On the other side of the door were more steps. These were even smaller and they ended abruptly in front of another metal door.

Frank twisted the knob and stepped inside. The others followed and crowded into the small space.

The group crept along the narrow hall single file, stopping every few feet when Frank would hold a finger to his lips. The rattle of pipes knocking against each other and the hiss of steam escaping the pipes caused an eerie, haunting sound.

They walked for several moments and then Frank abruptly stopped and pointed up. "There it is."

Annette gazed at the round hatch. On the front of the hatch was a metal wheel.

Frank climbed the rungs of the ladder, grasped the wheel and turned. Next, he tugged on the edge of the wheel and opened the hatch.

He hopped off the ladder and wiped his hands on the front of his pants. "Have a look," he said to Annette.

Annette climbed the rungs and stuck her head inside the hole for a quick look.

She pulled her head out of the hatch and hopped off the ladder. "I can do it. You say it leads to a catwalk inside the engine room?"

Frank nodded. "Yes."

Oscar, the second in command of security, shoved his hands in his pockets and studied the opening. "We will have to give you a weapon," he said.

"First, we have to come up with a plan," Annette said. "A two-prong assault on the engine room and bridge."

"Agreed." Andy nodded. "Let's head back upstairs to put a plan of attack together."

Chapter Sixteen

"You said Gloria left here a couple hours ago and she was going to track Millie down?" Liz asked.

"Yep," Dot nodded. "She was curious to find out if the person who went overboard was Danielle and if she was alright."

Ruth awoke from her sleep and resumed her position in front of the computer monitor.

Andrea leaned over Ruth's shoulder. "You see anything yet?"

"Quiet as a mouse, although I did see one thing I was going to run by Millie. It looked like someone delivered food to the engine room. At first, it looked like Danielle. Her hair was long and blonde, and she was wearing a uniform. She knocked on the door and then left."

"Did anyone open the door to get it?" Margaret asked.

"Yep. The door opened a few minutes later. All I could see was the top of someone's head as they knelt down, grabbed the tray and then a couple seconds later, the door closed. It was right around eleven-thirty."

The outer door to the suite flew open and Frances ran into the room. "The toilet in our cabin bathroom is overflowing!"

"What in the world?" Liz ran after a frantic Frances, following her to the suite across the hall.

Lucy shrugged. "Better them than us." She stepped out onto the balcony and gazed around. She remembered how Millie had used the selfie stick and her cell phone to peek into the captain's apartment directly below them.

Lucy tilted her head and peered over the side. It was a long way down. She wondered what it would feel like to fall off the balcony and into the water below. It would probably hurt...a lot.

Danielle had done it and survived. Perhaps it would depend on the fall itself and the angle of the person's body when they hit the water. She hoped she never had to find out.

Dot appeared at Lucy's side. "You're back," Lucy said.

Dot had gone down to guest services to check her account balance. "Whew! Guest services is a madhouse. People are pitching a fit that they can't use their cell phones, that the ship is sitting in the water. You name it, they're complaining."

She shook her head. "While I was standing there, someone called to say their toilet was overflowing in their cabin. What a mess!"

"Liz and Frances," Lucy grinned.

"Liz and Frances what?" Dot asked.

"It was Liz and Frances. Their toilet is overflowing."

"Good heavens." Dot shook her head. "I wonder how they managed that."

She changed the subject. "Gloria hasn't come back yet?"

"Nope." Lucy ran her fingers through her hair. "I'm beginning to worry about her. You don't think she concocted some brilliant rescue plan and struck out on her own..." Her voice trailed off. She didn't think her best friend would try to singlehandedly rescue the staff and crew, and capture the hijackers.

Andrea popped her head out the door. "I'm worried. Gloria should've come back by now. I think I'll see if I can track her down."

"I'll go with you," Lucy offered.

"Margaret, Ruth and I will hold down the fort," Dot said. She walked Lucy and Andrea to the door and left them with a word of warning. "Be careful. You never know if you'll run into one of the hijackers incognito."

Andrea and Lucy headed to the top deck first, scouring the lido deck, the buffet and the pool area before heading down one deck. They searched from top to bottom and end to end without a single sign of Gloria – or Millie.

"You don't think Gloria tracked down Millie and the two of them decided to embark on a seat-of-the-pants rescue mission and ended up getting caught, too?" Andrea voiced Lucy's same concerns.

Gloria might not act impulsively on her own, but if someone, namely Millie, who knew the ship like the back of her hand, was involved, it was possible. "I was thinking the same thing," Lucy admitted. "It's almost as if the two of them vanished into thin air."

They passed through Waves, the buffet area. The smell of sesame oil and garlic filled the air. Lucy stared at the array of food on display. "The smell is torture."

"Let's grab a bite to eat," Andrea suggested. The women walked over to the made-to-order Asian food station, *Bamboo Wok,* and joined the back of the line.

Andrea grabbed a large bowl, filled it with wonton noodles, along with baby corn, water chestnuts, julienne carrots and a small spoonful of bean sprouts.

"It looks delicious." Lucy grabbed a bowl from the tall stack, added some noodles and vegetables and rounded the corner.

"I'll have beef," Lucy decided.

"And I'll take shrimp," Andrea told the wok chef.

The chef nodded, and then coated two empty pans with cooking spray. In one pan, he dumped a large portion of uncooked sirloin strips. In the other, he put the shrimp and then placed both pans on the heat.

The meat sizzled and Lucy's mouth watered. Next, he dumped her bowl with the noodles and veggies inside the sizzling pan and mixed them with the beef before placing a cover on top.

He worked on Andrea's meal while Lucy's food cooked. When he finished cooking both dishes, he dumped Andrea's food into her bowl and then Lucy's lunch into her bowl.

Andrea reached for a set of chopsticks near the end of the counter. "Oh my gosh! This looks yummy."

The girls each grabbed a set of wrapped silverware and glass of iced tea before settling in at a table for two near the window.

After the girls prayed over their food, Lucy reached for her fork and Andrea removed the paper wrap from the chopsticks.

"The girls are missing out." Andrea squeezed a piece of shrimp between her chopsticks and popped it into her mouth. "I need to learn how to make this."

"Maybe you can have Alice give it a shot," Lucy suggested.

Alice was Andrea's former housekeeper who now lived with Andrea in her big, beautiful home in Belhaven, Michigan.

Andrea rolled her eyes. "Oh no! She would add so much spice to this dish it would singe the ends of my hair," she joked.

The girls gobbled their food, placed their dirty plates, napkins and silverware, along with the chopsticks Andrea had used, on top of their trays and stood. "We better head to the room to see if Gloria ever made it back."

The two women zig zagged through the throng of passengers and strolled past the packed pool as they made their way to the front of the ship.

The door to their suite was wide open. Next to the open door and lined up against one wall was a towering stack of suitcases.

Lucy stepped into the suite and pointed at the bags. "What is all this?"

Margaret hurried over. She glanced at Liz and Frances, who were standing out on the balcony. "Liz and Frances's suite flooded with water. They had to move out while maintenance cleans and dries the carpets."

Lucy's eyes widened in horror. "Move to where?"

"In with you," Margaret whispered. "The ship is full. There's nowhere else for them to go."

Andrea clutched her chest. "Does Gloria know?"

"Does Gloria know what?" Gloria, who had been MIA, suddenly appeared in the doorway.

Chapter Seventeen

"There you are!" Liz marched across the floor to the door. "This ship is a hunk of junk!" She whined. "Our bathroom and bedroom both flooded and maintenance made us move all of our stuff out until they can clean it up and dry the floors."

Frances crossed the room and tapped the top of the mound of suitcases. "I'm sorry Gloria. We had nowhere else to go."

"Don't apologize," Liz snapped. "It's all her fault we're on this rusty bucket of bolts in the first place!"

Gloria saw red as she had reached the upper limits of her tolerance level with her sister and Lucy, recognizing the look in her friend's eyes, took a step back.

Gloria shook her finger at her sister. "You! You invited yourself on this cruise in the first place so don't start on me about this being all my fault!"

She kicked the side of the luggage with the tip of her sandal. "If you don't watch it, I'm going to toss you and your crap out of my cabin and you can go sleep on the balcony for all I care."

Liz, on the receiving end of Gloria's wrath, shrunk back and then burst into tears. She wailed loudly at her younger sister's stern scolding.

Gloria, accustomed to her sister's extreme levels of drama, crossed her arms and rolled her eyes as she waited for the meltdown to taper off.

"You probably wish the hijackers had captured me," Liz sobbed.

Her sister smiled. "Now that's an idea."

The tears vanished. Liz lifted her head and stomped her foot. "You're so mean," she pouted.

"Come on, Liz. I was kidding!" Gloria, feeling guilty for snapping at her sister, quickly caved.

"If you stop with the drama, you can stay, but only if you behave yourself."

Frances grasped Liz's arm and tugged. "I'll make sure she straightens up." She led Liz to the balcony and away from the fuming Gloria.

Lucy quickly changed the subject. "Andrea and I have been looking for you. We were worried Millie and you had attempted a rescue on your own."

"No." Gloria shook her head. "I wish I could say we had managed a successful rescue mission, but we didn't." She waved them into Margaret's cabin. "I'll tell everyone what is going on in the other room."

The girls assembled in the suite next door: Gloria, Lucy, Andrea, Margaret, Dot and Ruth. Liz and Frances hovered out on the balcony, not daring to come back in...yet.

Gloria explained there were several staff being held against their will inside the bridge: Captain Armati, Staff Captain Vitale, Purser Donovan

Sweeney, along with Head of Security, Dave Patterson, Amit, the kitchen staff and finally the only woman they knew of, Ingrid Kozlov.

"We don't know how many captors there are. Danielle counted three, but there may have been more. She didn't have much time to look inside before one of them started chasing her and she fell off the side of the ship."

"She's lucky she survived," Dot said.

Gloria agreed. "Yes, she is. I asked her about it and she said it was the way she fell that saved her." She stiffened her back, pressed her arms close to her sides and lifted her head to demonstrate. "Straight down with toes pointed. And try not to panic," Gloria added.

Margaret shuddered. "Whew! Well, I don't plan on falling overboard."

"Me either," Gloria said. "Which is why I'm going to have a rope tied around me when they lower me to the deck below."

Ruth jerked her head and shifted her gaze away from the monitor as she stared at Gloria. "You're going to try to sneak into the captain's apartment?"

Gloria nodded. "Only long enough to place a mic inside and then sneak back out. Someone in the bridge is a mole and we have to figure out whom that someone is."

"But what if they catch you?" Dot asked.

"We can lower the phone first, to make sure the apartment is empty."

Lucy shifted her feet. "Why not someone else, namely security?"

"Because this is my suite and I want to do it," Gloria said.

Liz, her meltdown forgotten, overheard the conversation and made her way into the room. "You have lost your mind! You're not a spring chicken, Gloria. What if you break another bone…or worse yet, fall into the ocean and drown?"

Gloria shrugged. "Nah! It'll be over before you know it. I'm just waiting for Millie to get here." She turned to Ruth. "I thought I saw a mic in your bag of tricks."

Ruth nodded. "Yeah, I have one, but I'm not sure about this either," she said as she slid out of the chair and headed to the closet.

"My ears are burning," Millie strolled into the room, rope in hand. "For the record, I am totally against Gloria doing this but she insisted."

Gloria reached for the rope. "We need to get the phone set up first."

Millie plucked her phone out of her pocket while Andrea headed to the other suite to get the selfie stick.

The two women quickly assembled the makeshift spy camera, complete with a couple more pieces of duct tape.

Ruth returned and handed Gloria a small silver object. "This is it."

Millie finished tightening the screws on the end of the selfie stick. "Oh! I almost forgot. Here." She handed Gloria a long, metal rod. On one end was a hook.

Gloria turned it over in her hand. "This looks like a..."

"It's one of those hanger hooks, or as we used to call them, a shepherd's hook," Millie explained. "You can hook it onto the handrail and pull yourself to the balcony."

"Gotcha! I'm ready. Tie me up!"

Andrea groaned.

Dot shook her head.

Lucy snorted.

"I wish I could go," Ruth admitted.

"Maybe next time," Gloria grinned.

Millie held up what appeared to be a jumble of straps. She flipped them around a couple times. "I think I have this right. Slip your legs in here."

Gloria slipped her legs in the harness while Millie adjusted the back straps and then flung a black strap over each of her cousin's shoulders.

Millie shifted to the front, clicked the metal latches to the belt and tugged. "For a brief time, we had a high wire theatrics show and they used this harness to keep the performers safe."

"You don't have the show anymore?" Lucy asked.

Millie shook her head. "Nope. One of the latches broke. The performer fell onto the stage below and suffered a concussion." She gave Gloria a quick glance. "But they fixed the harness. It's as good as new."

Liz snorted and Gloria shot her a death look.

"I'll run the phone video," Dot offered and darted outside with the selfie stick. She eased it

243

over the edge of the balcony, keeping an eye on it to make sure it wasn't down too far and visible from the balcony below.

Dot pulled it back up, rewound the recording. Andrea and Lucy peeked over her shoulder to view the tape. "I caught a glimpse of someone walking around inside," Dot reported in a low voice.

While Dot spied on the apartment below, Millie inserted the rope through the harness ring, she knotted it several times and held both ends. The two women stepped out onto the balcony and stood near the rail to wait.

Millie turned to Dot. "Let's run another visual to see if the apartment is empty now."

Dot repeated the same steps, lowering the phone, attached to the selfie stick and then slowly making her way along the edge. She pulled it back up, quickly switched to replay and watched. "Nope. Still no go."

Gloria tugged on the harness straps nervously. "This waiting is torture." She stepped inside the suite and began pacing the floor, the metal hooks of the harness clanking noisily. "I hope they hurry up."

They waited another few minutes and Dot lowered the phone a third time. She walked along the edge of the balcony before pulling the phone back up, stepping inside the suite and then gazing at the screen. "Coast is clear," she whispered in a loud voice.

"Finally!" Millie handed Gloria the mic and then the hanger hook. She wrapped the two ends of the rope through the metal balusters and then wrapped it once around the bottom rail. "That should hold. I'll need some help lowering Gloria."

"I'll do it," Liz volunteered.

Gloria shook her head. "Not that I don't trust you, Liz, but I don't trust you." She glanced at

245

her friends. "Andrea and Margaret. Can you two help Millie?"

Liz crossed her arms and backed into the corner of the balcony to pout.

Millie turned her attention to Gloria. "Climb over the side and hang on. When the girls are certain they have a secure hold on the ropes, we'll lower you down," she whispered and held a finger to her lips. She pointed down.

Gloria gave her a thumbs up and then straddled the railing.

The color drained from Dot's face as she watched her friend cling to the side of the balcony. *What if the girls lost their grip and Gloria plunged into the sea below?* She couldn't remember if Gloria even knew how to swim.

It was too late to ask.

Millie, Margaret and Andrea gripped the ropes tightly as Gloria released her hold on the railing and quickly disappeared from sight.

The rope inched forward.

"Move up," Millie motioned them forward.

Lucy peered over the side of the rail and gazed at the top of Gloria's head. "A little more rope," she said.

The girls fed a little more rope and then tightened their grip. "And...she's in. Give it some slack."

The plan was for Gloria to place the mic just inside the apartment, high enough so Captain Armati's dog, Scout, wouldn't be able to reach it yet low enough so that no one would notice.

Lucy clasped her hands and started to pray as she gazed anxiously over the side.

Gloria climbed over the side of the rail, shepherd's hook in hand and made an "up" motion with her thumb.

"Back up, back up," Lucy flipped her hand, palm up and made an "up" motion.

Andrea, Margaret and Millie began tugging furiously on the rope.

Lucy grabbed another section and all four of them quickly pulled Gloria to the edge of the rail.

Gloria vaulted over the side of the balcony railing, lost her balance and fell on her rear, a grin spread across her face from ear to ear. The adrenaline rush caused her hands to shake and she fumbled with the safety gear hooks.

With the gear off, the girls stepped inside and closed the slider. "Well?"

"No one was in the apartment except for the cutest little dog. He was about this big." Gloria held her hands a few inches apart.

"Scout." A lump formed in Millie's throat and tears burned the back of her eyes. At least Scout was okay. She didn't dare dwell on Captain Armati lest she break down and start bawling.

Ruth shifted her gaze from the monitor to Gloria. "Whoops! I guess you'll need an orbiter and headphones."

She popped out of the seat and headed to the closet again, returning moments later with a large cone shaped device. Attached to the narrow end of the cone was an oblong black handle.

"Thanks." Millie slid the headphones over the top of her head, carried the cone shaped device out onto the balcony and set it in one of the deck chairs. Millie pointed the cone toward the railing and then stepped back inside.

Now that the first phase of their mission had been accomplished, the girls quickly grew bored.

"I'm hungry," Dot said.

"Me too," Margaret agreed.

Andrea tapped Ruth on the shoulder. "Lucy and I ate not long ago. Why don't you head out with the others and grab some lunch?"

Ruth blinked rapidly. "Whew! Yeah. I'm starting to get cross-eyed."

Andrea settled into the seat Ruth vacated and all of the girls, except for Lucy, who took over the listening device and Andrea, who monitored the computer screen, headed out to grab a bite to eat.

***

Boris Smirnov tapped the gun in the palm of his hand as he paced back and forth across the floor of the bridge. Time was running out. It was three o'clock in the afternoon and Majestic Cruise Lines had only three hours left to drop the duffel bag filled with fifty million dollars in unmarked bills on the helipad. If not, he vowed to begin killing the crew aboard Siren of the Seas, starting with one of the top dogs, either Captain Armati or the man in charge of the money, Purser Donovan Sweeney.

The plan had gone off without a hitch and Boris's Russian counterparts had done their part to ensure his team – and their weapons – had arrived onboard the ship undetected.

It was a shame some of his comrades would not live long enough to enjoy the spoils of their newfound wealth, but the less people alive to talk about the operation, the better. It also meant more money for Boris.

Boris wasn't sure yet where he would celebrate his newfound wealth. He was leaning toward settling in Cuba, but other southern Caribbean islands were tempting, as well.

Perhaps he would travel around to the various islands and then contemplate a permanent home while he sipped frozen margaritas on the beach and counted his millions.

The only "fly in the ointment" so to speak had been the young blonde who had scaled the side of the ship and caught a glimpse of Boris and his team. He wasn't sure how much the woman had seen and it gnawed at him.

In fact, it had bothered him so much; he had sent one of his men out into the ship to track her down. She had been wearing a staff uniform. Boris knew enough to know she was not one of the crew, but someone with a higher status, not to mention a lot of guts...or stupidity.

Boris smiled grimly. He had told his underling he was not to return to the bridge without the woman or else he would toss him overboard...not that the underling would live much longer anyway.

He had noted a brief flicker of recognition in the captain's eyes when the woman was spotted, but Captain Armati was a strong man and despite a beating, he had not divulged the woman's name.

When the captain regained consciousness, they would try again...

"Comrade!" A stocky man in dark clothing stopped short. He lifted his hand in salute.

Boris placed both hands behind his back. "Yes."

"We have word from the outside."

Boris Smirnov followed the man to the other side of the bridge and over to the radio controls. He handed Boris a sheet of paper. "The team onboard the yacht said this message just came in."

"We received your demand for fifty million dollars in exchange for the release of our ship, along with the safe return of both our crew and passengers. We need another twelve hours to secure the funds and reach the ship for drop off. Please respond."

The message was signed, "Ted Danvers, CEO."

Boris crumpled the sheet in a ball and threw it across the room. "Incompetence!" he roared. He strode down the hall and into Captain Armati's apartment.

When Boris reached the bar area, he pulled out a half-empty bottle of vodka, unscrewed the cap and took a big swig. He wiped his mouth with the back of his hand before slamming the bottle down on the counter.

The other two hijackers stared uneasily at one another but no one dared approach Boris in his current state.

Chapter Eighteen

Ivan Gusev stood just outside the bridge and stared at the closed door. *Where to start looking for the girl? There was a chance she had been injured during the fall, which would mean she had been taken to medical.*

He made his way down to guest services and when he reached the front of the long line, he approached the petite brunette behind the counter. She looked frazzled and he knew why. All of the people around him that were waiting in line were grumbling about the lack of internet and phone connection. Not only that, the passengers had noticed the ship was not moving.

Nikki Tan swiped the stray strand of hair out of her eyes and smiled at the tall, broad shouldered man in front of her. "Can I help you?"

"Yes. I am looking for the ship's doctor. I feel...chest pains." Boris clutched his chest for emphasis.

Nikki's eyes widened and she reached for the phone. "I can call for one of the medical staff to come assist you."

"No!" Boris shouted and then lowered his voice. "I mean, no. I can go there on my own if you tell me how to get there."

Nikki leaned over the counter and pointed at the bank of elevators on the other side of the desk. "Take the elevators to deck two. Exit the elevators, turn left and go to the very back of the ship."

"Thank you." Boris smiled and stepped away from the desk as he headed to the bank of elevators.

***

Danielle fidgeted on the examination table, wishing she were anywhere but here. Although she was a little sore from the impact of hitting the water, she felt fine. She had grown weary of Doctor Gundervan and his staff hovering over her.

She glanced at the clock on the wall. Ten more minutes and she would be free to leave, at least that was what the good doctor had promised.

Danielle kicked the bottom of the examination table with the heel of her sopping wet sneaker as she plucked at her damp work shirt. All she'd been trying to do was help and the only thing she'd accomplished was to be on the receiving end of a stern reprimand courtesy of Andy, who had just stormed out of the medical center.

Andy had been madder than a wet hornet and informed her she was on restriction indefinitely.

Danielle glanced at the purple welt on the side of her arm. She was going to have a humdinger of a bruise, thanks to the bridge's windowsill she'd managed to crash into on the way down. At least the hijacker, who had taken a pot shot at her...well, several pot shots, had missed.

Doctor Gundervan emerged from the front. "Well, young lady, if you're sure you're feeling alright, you're free to go. I suggest you head back to your cabin and get some rest."

Danielle slid off the table. "Sweet! I'm a little sore but with the bottle of pills you gave me, I should be good as new. If not, I have your number," she joked.

Doctor Gundervan walked Danielle to the door and held it open. "I would like you to check in with me later this evening to let me know how you're feeling," he said.

"Ten four." Danielle gave a small salute before stepping out into the hall. She was a little sorer than she cared to admit and slowly limped down the hall.

When she reached the end of the hall, she changed her mind, realizing she would need some water to take the pills. She half thought about using the bathroom tap water but quickly nixed the idea.

Danielle pushed the "up" button on the elevator and stepped inside.

Out of nowhere, a burly man with sandy blonde hair stuck his hand between the elevator doors to prevent them from closing. He stepped inside.

She gave him a quick glance before she pushed the button for the eleventh floor.

The man pushed the button for deck ten.

Something about him caused the hair on the back of Danielle's neck to stand up and she took a step back.

Watch your back, Danielle. Casey's voice echoed in Danielle's ear. She instinctively reached inside her soggy pants pocket and rubbed the small, smooth stone between her index finger and thumb.

It had been almost a year now since Casey's death...one long, painful year and her heart still ached, even now.

Perhaps the fall had been more traumatizing than she initially thought.

Danielle crossed her arms and clenched her jaw as she focused on the blinking elevator numbers, willing them to move faster.

Get off the elevator, Danielle. Casey's voice warned. Danielle had heard his voice several times over the past year as he warned her of impending danger. So far, his warnings had always been spot on.

She impulsively jabbed a lower floor button, hoping to get off as quickly as possible. She was in luck. The elevator stopped on deck nine.

The doors opened and there were several people standing outside the elevator, waiting to get on.

Danielle darted off the elevator.

The stranger followed her off.

Danielle picked up the pace as she hurried to the stairs, taking the steps two at a time. Her aching body groaned in protest at the exertion.

She didn't look behind her...she didn't need to. She knew the stranger was following her!

He's right behind you Pickle. Pickle had been Casey's pet name for his older sister, his only sibling, who always seemed to get in a pickle.

She quickly blinked back the tears that stung the back of her eyes and focused on putting as much distance as possible between her and the sinister stranger, but it was too late.

Danielle felt a sharp pain in the back of her head and then her world went dark.

Ivan Gusev picked up the blonde, easily flung her over his left shoulder and ascended the one flight of stairs to the bridge.

"Hey! Everything alright, dude?" A young man wearing a heavy metal t-shirt and black swim trunks approached Ivan.

Ivan slowly turned. He had a split second to decide what to do. "Yes. My girlfriend, she have a few too many, you know?" He tipped his head back and lifted his hand as if guzzling an invisible drink.

"Ah." The young man smiled and nodded. "Cool." He waved and headed down the hall.

Ivan watched until the young passenger disappeared before turning and rapidly walking to the door that led to the bridge. The last thing he needed was to run into anyone else, especially a crewmember who might recognize the unconscious woman draped over his shoulder.

When he got to the door, he rapped loudly. The door swung open and Ivan, still carrying Danielle, disappeared inside.

***

"Oh my gosh!" Andrea stared at the computer screen in disbelief. She clicked the mouse over the play button and slid it to the left to rewind. "Check this out."

Lucy shifted the right headphone off her ear and gazed at the computer screen. "That looks like Millie's friend. What's her name?"

"Danielle. A man just carried Danielle into the bridge!" Andrea jumped out of her chair. "We've got to do something!"

"Wait! I hear something!" Lucy adjusted the headphones and cranked up the volume.

"Put her there!" A man with a thick Russian accent spoke. "We will find out what she knows once she comes to."

Lucy heard a soft moan and could only surmise the person moaning was Danielle.

"We're back!" Liz breezed into the suite and swept off to the side, accompanied by the other girls.

"Shh!" Lucy put a finger to her lips and pointed at the headphones. She was amazed at the clarity of the small listening device.

The others tiptoed into the room and hovered around Lucy.

Andrea clicked the back arrow on the video and then paused it at the point where the man, carrying Danielle, reached the door.

Lucy shook her head. "It's quiet." She looked at Andrea. "Show them what you have."

All eyes turned to the computer monitor. Andrea pressed the "play" button and they watched in horror as the man approached the bridge carrying an unconscious woman. He rapped three times on the door, it opened and the two of them disappeared inside.

"That was Danielle," Millie muttered.

Annette, who had met up with the girls near the buffet area, grimaced. "Yeah. They must have thought she'd seen too much inside the bridge before she plunged into the ocean."

"Wh-what do you think will happen to her?" Dot asked.

Millie frowned. "They aren't going to keep her around. My guess is they will try to find out what she knows, who she told and then get rid of her."

Gloria began to pace. "We need to do something. We need to figure out who the mole is, come up with a plan and rescue everyone!"

"I heard something while you were gone. It was a man's voice." Lucy looked at Millie. "Maybe you'll recognize it." She handed the headphones to Millie and Millie slid them on.

Lucy replayed the tape to the spot where she recalled hearing the voice.

Millie listened quietly and then her mouth dropped open. "Oh my gosh! I-I think I might have an idea who the mole is!"

"We're running out of time. Danielle is in big trouble. These guys mean business," Millie added.

The wheels were spinning in Millie's head. The only way to access the bridge was through the captain's apartment and in through the slider.

Now that the mic was in place, they would be able to tell if anyone was around. Still, it was risky. They needed a visual of the apartment, to see what was going on. Otherwise, whoever went in could very well walk right into a trap.

"I can borrow one of the rolled fire escape ladders from maintenance," Annette suggested. "Attach it to the side of Gloria's balcony, roll it down and access the captain's balcony."

Gloria, who had been staring at the computer screen, looked up. "You mean instead of hooking me to a harness and swinging me over the side of the balcony, we could have used a ladder?" she asked incredulously, her gaze shifting to her cousin.

Millie shrugged. "In the heat of the moment, I didn't think about that. It's not like I work in maintenance."

Annette hustled to the door. "I'm going to get the ladder and Andy, along with maintenance and security."

She returned a short time later with Andy and Oscar, both of whom had been monitoring the mic Annette had placed inside the vent outside the engine room. Last, but not least, was Frank, the head of maintenance.

"Oscar is going into the apartment. Annette is the only one small enough to crawl through the vent," Andy said. "Security and the undercover agents will be in charge of the rest of the rescue mission."

He gave Millie a stern look. "You..." He shifted his gaze to include all the girls. "Are to stay out of this and leave it to the professionals."

Millie frowned.

Gloria sighed heavily.

"Too bad we don't have a gun," Lucy said. "If the hijackers were able to kidnap Danielle, any one of us could be in danger."

"Oh no!" Andy shook his head. "The last thing we need is for one of you to accidentally shoot yourself."

"I would never shoot myself or anyone else...that I don't want to," Lucy replied indignantly.

"She's a weapons expert," Gloria said.

"A sharp shooter," Ruth added.

"This isn't your run-of-the-mill granny," Margaret agreed.

"No guns for the girls," Oscar said firmly. "Except for Annette."

"Annette is taking on the engine room?" Millie asked incredulously.

A man Millie hadn't noticed before stepped forward and nodded. He was the same one Millie had seen hanging around guest services and she had approached earlier to ask if he needed assistance....John. "From her vantage point in the vent, she will have the element of surprise. Otherwise, the engine room is basically impenetrable and we won't have a shot at securing the area."

Oscar stepped forward to introduce the man. "Jim Kelly, special operations agent and first in command."

Jim Kelly spoke again. "The cruise line is unable to meet the demands of the hijackers. We know they will carry through on their threat to kill their hostages so we must move now."

He turned to Oscar. "Let's go back to the temporary command post to run through the plan one last time. "These are the women who set up surveillance in Captain Armati's apartment?"

"Yes," Andy nodded.

Kelly hardened his jaw. "Under no circumstances are any of you to interfere with the rescue of the staff and crew. Is that understood?"

"Or else what?" Millie challenged.

"I'll have you arrested," Jim Kelly replied.

Chapter Nineteen

Annette checked the safety lock on the gun and then tucked it into the waistband of her pants. She stared at the ladder and then lifted her gaze as she studied the opening of the vent. "Here goes nothing. Wish me luck."

Felippe, one of the ship's security officers, nodded. "Shoot 'em dead, Annette."

He watched as Annette climbed the ladder and disappeared inside the vent before quietly making his way down the narrow hall to join the armed agents hiding behind a row of large, square mechanical boxes directly across from the engine room door.

***

Annette lowered onto her hands and knees and cautiously crept along the inside of the metal vent. It had been years since the last time she'd gone in under cover and attempted to take out a criminal element.

A rush of adrenaline surged through her body and her heart began to race. She prayed her aim was still dead on. There would be no second chance. As soon as the hijackers figured out where the gunfire was coming from, her cover would be blown and it would be all over.

Based on what limited information she'd been given, there were four crew and three hijackers inside the engine room. Annette's gun clip had plenty of bullets, although the hijackers would have at least triple that.

Annette reached the end of the vent, slipped her fingernail under the edge of the cover and gently pulled it off. The opening was small but still large enough for her to not only get a visual of the exit door, but also get the tip of her gun through. It would have to be enough.

She studied the room carefully and discovered she was in luck. All four of the ship's engine crew were seated in front of the computer monitors while two hijackers stood guard behind them.

Annette's eyes darted around the room as she searched frantically for the third accomplice. He was nowhere in sight and she was out of time. She aimed her gun and pointed it at the exit door.

Ping! Ping!

"What was that?" The hijackers darted across the room and over to the door. The first hijacker to reach the door pushed it open and peeked around the corner.

Ping! Someone on the other side of the door fired off another shot.

The two hijackers, under fire from the outside, flattened their bodies against the wall and began to back into the engine room.

Unfortunately, for them, this put them directly into Annette's line of fire.

Annette narrowed her gaze and squeezed the trigger of the gun in rapid succession. *Pop! Pop!*

Two for two. She was certain she'd hit both of them on her first try but fired off a couple more rounds just to be safe.

The room erupted in chaos as the third hijacker; the one Annette hadn't been able to get a visual on, materialized from behind the row of computer equipment.

"Stay there!" He waved his gun at the hostages, who quickly dropped back into their seats.

Annette turned the gun and aimed at the last standing hijacker. As if feeling her eyes on him, he shifted his gaze and their eyes met as he spied her through the vent hole. He lifted his assault rifle.

It was now or never. *Pop! Pop, Pop!* Annette fired off three quick shots, hitting him in his trigger arm, his shoulder and his right leg.

The man stumbled back and lost his grip on the gun.

Two of the ship's crew quickly overpowered the third hijacker while the other two crewmembers lunged at the injured hijackers and easily wrestled the weapons from them.

Annette studied the scene closely. When she was certain the ship's crew had the situation under control and the hijackers were no longer armed, she wiggled backward out of the vent.

When she reached the opening, she slid out of the hole and down the narrow ladder, still clutching the gun.

Annette strode down the narrow hall that led to the engine room. A small movement caught her eye. "Hello?"

Felippe, along with three men dressed in street clothes, crawled out of the narrow space behind a row of metal equipment.

The men quickly raced into the engine room. Annette followed behind, stopping just inside the doorway. She had managed to hit all three of them in the leg, the arm and the shoulder, right where she'd aimed.

"Nice shots," Felippe said admiringly.

Annette nodded. "Thanks. We better get medical down here to get them bandaged up and then take them to the cooler."

She unclipped the radio from her belt and handed it to one of the hijackers, all the while keeping her gun pointed at his temple. "But before we do, radio your comrades and tell them they need to get down here. You have an emergency!"

***

The girls huddled around the monitor and watched the scene unfold in front of the engine room door.

After the undercover agents, along with Annette and Felippe, disappeared inside the engine room, Ruth switched screens to the one outside the bridge.

The door to the bridge flew open and two tall muscular men burst out of the bridge.

Jim Kelly, the special agent, along with two of the ship's armed security crew, fought with the hijackers in a desperate attempt to wrestle their guns away.

A third gunman raced out of the bridge and rushed toward the melee underway.

Millie gasped and quickly covered her mouth. "Oh no!"

The third hijacker tackled special agent Kelly. The men fought hard and it looked as if the criminal was gaining the upper hand when suddenly his body grew limp. He stared sightlessly at Agent Kelly and then closed his eyes.

Jim Kelly shoved the man's body to the side and came face-to-face with Captain Armati, who was holding a nine iron and breathing heavily.

Captain Armati dropped the golf club on the floor. "What took you so long?"

Millie pried her eyes from the screen and jogged across the suite as she made her way out onto the balcony where Oscar was waiting. "Time to go!"

Oscar flipped the fire ladder over the edge of Gloria's balcony and scampered down the ladder. He quickly vaulted over the side and onto the balcony below...Captain Armati's balcony.

The room was empty except for Captain Armati's Yorkie, Scout, who darted over and began pawing at his leg.

Oscar reached down and patted his head. "I'll be right back, fella, but first, I have to take care of some business."

Oscar started across the room as he headed toward the bridge when he heard a thumping noise coming from behind a closed door on the other side of the captain's compact living room.

He made his way over to the door and slowly turned the knob, all the while clutching his gun in his right hand.

He peered around the corner and lowered his gaze. Bound and gagged inside the captain's bathroom were Dave Patterson, Head of Security, Purser Donovan Sweeney and Amit.

Oscar met Patterson's eyes and he smiled. "Hang tight. I'll be right back, boss."

Oscar mentally counted the captives in the closet. There were only three people unaccounted for: Captain Armati, Staff Captain Vitale and one more...the mole, aka, Russian born Ingrid Kozlov!

Oscar cautiously eased open the door that connected Captain Armati's apartment to the bridge. He heard a commotion off to one side and opened the door a little wider for a better look.

"Oh no you don't!" Staff Captain Antonio Vitale was trying desperately to keep a firm grip on Ingrid Kozlov's waist. Ingrid elbowed Captain Vitale in the groin, which caused him to release his hold.

Seizing her opportunity, Ingrid yanked on the handle of the bridge's side door as she attempted to flee.

Oscar flung the door all the way open and raced across the bridge. "Freeze or I'll shoot!"

Ingrid let go of the doorknob, her arms falling to her sides.

Oscar lifted the gun and with great pleasure pointed it at the back of Ingrid Kozlov's head. "Don't move or I will gladly blow your head off."

The hall leading to the bridge and the bridge itself exploded in a beehive of activity as security and secret agents cuffed the hijackers, including Ingrid Kozlov, and quickly escorted them to the holding cells in the bottom of the ship.

Oscar raced back into the captain's apartment to free Purser Donovan Sweeney, Dave Patterson and Amit.

Captain Armati and Staff Captain Vitale, along with the crew in the engine room, quickly restored communications, fired up the ship's engines and propulsion system and the ship began to move.

After the ship was in motion, Captain Armati contacted Majestic Cruise Lines' headquarters to let them know the crew had regained control of the ship while the special agents phoned U.S. authorities in Miami to inform them of the ship's status.

Millie couldn't stand it a minute longer. She ran out of Gloria's suite, down the hall and to the bridge. The other girls trailed behind.

When she reached the bridge, she crossed the threshold, her eyes scanning the room as she reassured herself that Captain Armati, Staff

Captain Vitale, Amit, Dave Patterson and Donovan Sweeney were all safe.

"Where's Danielle?" she asked Dave Patterson. "I don't see Danielle."

Patterson shuffled across the room and put an arm around Millie's shoulder. "I'm sorry Millie. Danielle was throwing such a fit, the hijackers took her out right after she regained consciousness. I don't know what happened to her," he admitted.

Millie tilted her head to study Patterson's expression. "I...do you think they killed her?" she asked fearfully.

"Surely they didn't kill her." Her lower lip began to quiver. "I would give anything to hear her voice again."

"Like give up your lower bunk," a familiar voice behind her teased.

Millie spun around and came face-to-face with a grinning Danielle.

Annette was directly behind her. "We found her tied up in the corner of the engine room with a piece of duct tape covering her mouth. Guess they couldn't handle her either," Annette joked.

Danielle gave her a dark look. "What a bunch of nincompoops. Why, you'd think they were afraid of lil ole me."

Millie grabbed Danielle's hand and pulled her close. "See what I have to put up with?" She eyed Andy and hugged Danielle.

Scout ran circles around the bridge, excited to see Millie, the captain and the rest of the crew.

Gloria bent down and picked up the small dog. "Why, aren't you the cutest little pup in the world? I should take you home. Mally and Puddles would love you!" she gushed.

"Ah, you must be Millie's cousin," Staff Captain Vitale correctly guessed. "Would you like a brief tour of the bridge since you're here?"

Gloria's face brightened. "That would be awesome."

Gloria, Liz and the others followed Staff Captain Vitale to the other side of the bridge.

"Millie, are you there?" Millie's two-way radio went off. It was Nikki down in guest services.

Millie unclipped the radio and lifted it to her lips. "Yes, Nikki. The ship is back on track and we're on our way to..." She turned to face Captain Armati and her heart skipped a beat as she gazed into his eyes.

The captain smiled and put both hands behind his back. "St. Croix. We shall arrive tomorrow morning after we put the 'pedal to the metal' as you Americans like to say."

"Captain Armati said we will dock in St. Croix in the morning."

Nikki groaned and Millie could sense the young woman's frustration. She shifted her gaze from the captain to Andy. "Can someone make an announcement? The crew, staff and especially the passengers have been anxious."

"Of course," Captain Armati said. "Tell Nikki I will handle it."

"Captain Armati is going to make an announcement via the intercom." Millie lowered the volume on her radio and clipped it to her belt.

Millie turned her attention to the captain as she narrowed her eyes and studied his face. There was a noticeable purple bruise on his left cheek and dried blood near the corner of his mouth.

She instinctively reached out to touch the side of his face before jerking her hand back. "The hijackers roughed you up."

Captain Armati touched the corner of his mouth with his index finger and wiggled his jaw. "It's a little battle wound. I'll be fine," he assured her.

"I appreciate your concern, Millie." His eyes sparkled when they met Millie's eyes and a wave of heat rushed through her veins.

He tilted his head and lowered his voice. "Do you think we can reschedule our ruined dinner date?"

Millie's face grew hot. "Y-yes. I...Yes." She nodded and pressed her lips tightly together, fearful she was about to blurt out something embarrassing like "I love you."

Andy strolled over and lightly tapped Millie's shoulder, bringing her back to earth and her senses. "We better get back to work," he whispered in her ear.

Danielle studied the large computer screen in the center of the bridge. "Maybe I don't want to work security after all. I'm going to apply for the next open position in the bridge...maybe Ingrid's!"

"That would be disastrous," Annette predicted.

Andy shook his head and smiled at Danielle. "Follow me, young lady. Your vacation is over," he teased.

"Vacation?" Danielle gasped as she followed Millie and Andy from the bridge. "You think being shot at by hijackers, falling off the side of the ship, being knocked unconscious by a brute and then tied up was a vacation?"

Gloria, Andrea and Lucy turned to go. "Ladies!" the captain stopped them.

Gloria cringed and slowly turned, certain they were about to get a tongue-lashing.

Captain Armati took a step forward and extended his hand as he eyed each of them carefully, his gaze settling on Gloria. "So you are the infamous cousin Gloria." He smiled.

"Y-yes sir." She wasn't sure what to do so she lifted her hand to her forehead and saluted him.

"At ease," he teased. "It's a pleasure to meet you. Thank you for participating in our rescue."

Lucy muscled her way closer. "Hey! What about us? What are we? Chopped liver?"

Lucy thrust her hand out. "Lucy Carlson, at your service."

"It is a pleasure to meet you, Lucy Carlson."

Lucy pointed to Andrea. "This is Andrea Malone."

Captain Armati lifted a brow. "Andrea Malone. Has anyone ever told you that you look a lot like Danielle?"

"As a matter of fact..." she shook his hand.

Annette and Amit hovered off to the side while the captain talked to Millie's family.

Captain Armati looked solemnly at Annette and then the corners of his mouth turned up as he grinned. "Ah, Annette. Your cover is blown," he teased. "When the dust settles, Millie will corner you for a full confession," he warned.

Annette rolled her eyes. "I'm afraid you're right." She glanced at her watch. "I better get back to the kitchen." She turned to Amit. "C'mon Amit. The party is over."

Amit scrunched his brows. "What cover? What party?"

Annette linked her arm through Amit's arm. "It's a long, boring story and one we don't have time for right now. As a matter of fact, we may never have time."

Chapter Twenty

Gloria set Scout down and he pranced around. "What will you do about the woman…what is her name?"

"Ingrid. Ingrid Kozlov." Captain Armati's expression grew grim. "I am disappointed in myself. I thought I vetted my people better than that."

Staff Captain Vitale leaned an elbow on the computer monitor. "Don't be so hard on yourself, captain. I thought the same thing."

Gloria slowly shook her head. "Happens all the time. Greed. Power. It sounds as if she just let it suck her in."

Andrea gazed around the bridge. "We better head back to the cabin. The girls are probably chomping at the bit to find out what happened."

Captain Armati nodded. "And I have an announcement to make."

Dave Patterson and Oscar, who had been silently standing off to the side, said their good-byes to the captain. "We'll brief the security staff within the hour," Patterson promised.

The girls headed up the stairs while Patterson and Oscar, accompanied by several undercover agents, headed down.

As the girls stepped into Gloria, Andrea and Lucy's suite, they were swarmed by Margaret, Dot, Ruth, Liz and Frances.

"It was a spectacular rescue mission," Ruth gushed. "I recorded it all so we can watch it again when we get home. Maybe we can pick up a few pointers for future reference."

Gloria sank into the chair, leaned her head back and closed her eyes. Her head was swimming as she tried to digest all that had happened.

Dot slid into the chair next to Ruth and glanced at the computer screen. She leaned in and pointed at the monitor. "Is that what I think it is?"

"What is what?" Lucy made her way over. "Ruth! Are you spying on the post office?"

"What?" Ruth defended herself. "Without internet access, I haven't been able to keep track of the place."

Kenny Webber, Ruth's right hand man and rural route carrier, waved to the camera. Ruth waved back, as if he could see her. "I have to keep an eye on the temp." She shook her head. "These fill-in people. You gotta watch 'em."

Ruth pointed at the yellow pad sitting next to her laptop. "I'm taking notes."

"Too bad I can't see what's going on at the restaurant," Dot said as she stared at the screen. "I could check up on Ray and the Morris's."

Ray was Dot's husband. He, along with Johnnie and Rose Morris, were holding down the fort and running the restaurant while Dot was on her much-needed vacation.

"Oh, we can." Ruth tapped the keyboard a few times, grabbed the mouse and shifted the pointer.

With a couple quick clicks, the screen switched from the inside of the post office to the parking lot, which included a view of Belhaven's main street and the front of Dot's restaurant.

"Check it out," Gloria grinned and leaned in. "Can you get any closer?"

"Sure." Ruth rolled the wheel on the mouse and the camera zoomed in.

The girls huddled around as they stared through the front window of the restaurant.

"There's Ray," Margaret said.

"Yep. Looks like he's carrying a cheeseburger and an order of onion rings," Dot said.

"Yum. A burger sure does sound good." Frances patted her stomach.

A heavy-set woman with curly black hair, a wide grin on her face and carrying a pot of coffee passed by the window, stopped at a table near the front and poured coffee into a diner's coffee cup.

She set the pot on the edge of the table and stuck a hand on her hip. The girls could see her mouth moving ninety miles an hour.

"There's Rose," Ruth said.

Dot grinned. "She's a talker. That woman – she can weave a tale or two."

"Looks like she's settling right in," Gloria commented.

They watched a few more moments and then Ruth switched the camera back to the interior of the post office.

The intercom sounded and Gloria jumped as a voice boomed over the cabin speakers.

"Ladies and Gentleman. This is Captain Niccolo Armati speaking to you from the bridge. I would like to update you on the status of our cruise. We are moving full steam ahead to our next port stop – the island of St. Croix. We will arrive right on schedule and will dock in the port town of Frederiksted. After we clear customs, you are free to disembark the ship and enjoy your day on the island. Tomorrow's forecast is perfect, with temperatures in the mid-80s, sunny skies and gentle trade winds."

He went on. "In celebration of my return as captain of Siren of the Seas after an extended leave, we are offering complimentary beverages in all of our bars and lounges for the next hour. Have a wonderful afternoon and evening. Arrivederci."

"We better beat the crowd." Liz, with Frances hot on her heels, ran from the room.

"Free drinks!" Margaret sprung from the bed and darted to the door. "I'm on it!"

Andrea groaned. "I better supervise. Plus, I've been dying to try one of those yellow birds."

"Not without me!" Ruth scrambled from her chair and trailed behind.

Dot shrugged. "If you can't beat 'em, join 'em."

Gloria and Lucy, the last two left in the suite, stared at each other. "Well, Lucy. Another adventure under our belt."

The women wandered into the hall. "Do you think anyone back home will believe it?"

"Probably not." Gloria glanced at Liz and Frances' luggage. "Shoot! I almost forgot Liz and Frances were staying in our suite. Maybe Frank, the head of maintenance, will take pity on us and put a rush on getting their suite cleaned so they can move back in."

The rest of the day sailed by and after sipping frothy concoctions and stopping by the buffet for a late lunch, they ran into Dave Patterson near the bar in the back of the ship.

He told them authorities had captured the crew aboard the yacht that was waiting nearby for the hijackers.

When the girls returned to their suites a couple hours later, they found a note shoved under their door. It was from Millie, telling them she was saving them front row seats for the evening's headliner, Julio Marchan, a world-renowned magician.

The show was fascinating and Gloria thoroughly enjoyed Mr. Marchan's performance. She was stumped by his ability to make people disappear from the stage and then reappear in the upper balcony wearing different clothes.

After the show ended, Millie snuck over to let the girls know everything was back to normal and to thank them for all their help. "What are you doing tomorrow? she asked.

"Honestly, I haven't thought that far ahead," Gloria admitted. "I'm sure we'll get off the ship, though. It will be nice to have both feet on solid ground."

"Andy gave me part of the day off so maybe I can hang out with you guys," Millie suggested.

"We would love that," Lucy said sincerely. "I'm sure Liz and Frances would like that, too."

"Depends on how much sleep I get tonight," Liz grumbled. "Last I checked, maintenance was still working on our suite so I guess we're gonna have to bunk with Gloria and sleep on rollaway beds."

Millie raised a brow. "I'll give Frank a call to see if he can have maintenance bring in a few more floor dryers to speed it up."

"Whatever you can do to get Liz out of my suite and back into her own would be greatly appreciated," Gloria said.

The girls agreed to meet Millie at the gangway at nine-thirty the next morning.

Afterwards, they wandered out of the theater and headed to the ice cream station for a sweet treat.

Gloria popped the last bite of chocolate ice cream cone in her mouth and wiped her hands on the front of her shorts. "I'm whupped."

"Me too," Dot agreed. "We're going to have a busy day tomorrow. Maybe we should hit the hay early."

The girls wandered back to their suites and took turns in the bathroom getting ready for bed. Gloria and Andrea slipped out onto the balcony where they spied the portable ladder Oscar had used to gain access to Captain Armati's apartment.

"Guess we can take this off now," Andrea quipped as she reached for the hooks.

Lucy slipped out onto the balcony to join Gloria and Andrea. "Maybe you can take it home as a souvenir," she said. "In case you get trapped out on the roof again."

Gloria waved a hand dismissively. "That was eons ago."

Liz was the last straggler to make it back to the suite and the last to get ready for bed. She grumbled the entire time about having to sleep on a rollaway bed and how the cruise line should comp her with a free cruise to make up for all the trouble she'd gone through.

"You?" Gloria said. "What about me?"

The girls finally shut the interior lights off and all five of them were rocked to sleep by the gentle rolling waves and the soothing motion of the ocean.

Chapter Twenty-One

Millie stopped by Cat's cabin early the next morning before heading up to meet Gloria, Liz and their friends for a beach day in St. Croix.

She lightly tapped on the door and waited.

She had almost given up when the door opened a crack. "Cat?"

Cat opened the door wider. "Hi Millie. What's up?"

Millie noticed Cat was dressed in street clothes. "I thought I would stop by to see if you'd like to join my cousins and me for a day at the beach."

Cat lowered her gaze. "No. I mean, I have a few hours off but I have some things to take care of," she said.

"Like what?" Millie asked.

"Oh...stuff." Cat shrugged.

Millie placed the palm of her hand on the door. "Can I come in for a minute?"

Cat nodded. "Sure." She stepped to the side and Millie made her way in, closing the door behind her. "Is your roommate gone?"

Cat nodded. "Lila left a little while ago."

Cat's cabin was identical to Millie and Danielle's cabin. Inside the cabin were a set of bunk beds, a small desk with one chair and two sets of closets.

Millie eased into the desk chair and shifted so she faced her friend. "Cat, I'm worried about you. You haven't left the ship since returning from the hospital. You can't...you shouldn't have to live like this."

Cat eased onto the edge of the bunk bed and studied her fingernails as Millie spoke.

Millie pressed on. "I'm here to help, so is Annette and everyone else. Are you afraid Jay is going to escape prison again and hunt you down?"

Cat clenched her fists and nodded. "Yes," she whispered. "I can't sleep at night. All I can see is his face...that look." Her shoulders shook. "I am so afraid now, it's hard to function."

"You have PTSD," Millie guessed. "Post-traumatic stress disorder."

Millie sprung from the chair and knelt down in front of Cat. She tilted her head and looked into her friend's eyes. "You need more than a shoulder to cry on. You need professional help. Will you let me talk to Doctor Gundervan to find out if there's some way we can get you the help you need?"

Cat shrugged. "What if they think I'm cuckoo or something and decide to fire me?"

Millie squeezed her friend's hand. "They will not think you're crazy, Cat. You have been through a lot. The crew on this ship knows that better than anyone, even better than your own family."

She paused to let her words sink in. "So, will you let me see if we can find help?"

Cat was quiet for a long moment as she considered Millie's offer. Finally, she lifted her head. "Yes. Yes please."

A tear trickled down Cat's cheek and then another.

Cat began to sob uncontrollably. Millie wrapped her arm around her friend's shoulders and silently prayed for healing.

Finally, Millie ran into the tiny bathroom and brought back a roll of toilet paper. She unrolled a large section, tore it off and handed it to Cat, who wiped her cheeks and blew her nose. "Thanks for the ear, Millie."

Millie wiped her own eyes. "We're gonna get you the help you need, Cat. I promise," she said.

Before this day is over, I will have an answer, Millie silently vowed.

She glanced at her watch. "Hang in there, my friend. We will get through this together."

She hustled over to the door, grabbed the door handle and then turned back. "Are you sure you don't want to go with us?" she asked hopefully.

Cat shook her head. "Maybe next time," she whispered.

***

"You said that Dot, Margaret and Ruth are already off the ship?" Gloria asked as they dinged their keycards and shuffled down the gangway.

"Positive." Lucy nodded. "Dot called down to talk to Millie last night after they went to their room and she suggested a really cool out of the way beach where we could all hang out, away from the crowds. She said someone would have to get there early to save enough lounge chairs and tables for all of us."

Gloria didn't have time to answer. She spotted Millie standing off to the side, looking carefree and tropical in her pink beach cover, flip-flops and large straw hat.

"Right on time." Millie grinned and hugged each of them as they made their way over. "Annette and Amit pulled a few strings and packed a picnic lunch for all of us." She tapped on the top of a beach cart sitting next to her.

"This way." Millie grabbed the cart handle and began walking down the dock. When they reached the end, she turned right.

They strolled along the shoreline, passing by row after row of bright blue beach loungers and cruise ship passengers who were already soaking up the sun.

Gloria could hear the faint beat of steel drums. She looked up. Overhead, the palm trees swayed. It was the perfect Caribbean beach day.

They reached a long stretch of massive rocks that jutted out of the ocean. Andrea helped Millie carry the beach cart up and over the top of the rocks.

Off in the distance. Gloria caught a glimpse of Dot waving a bright red scarf in the air.

As they got closer, Gloria grinned when she realized why Dot, Margaret and Ruth had gone on ahead.

"Surprise!" Everyone yelled and pointed to a large white sign tied to two palm trees. The sign read, "Castaway Party."

On top of the picnic table was a pink cast, cut in half. Gloria burst out laughing.

Millie wrinkled her nose, a confused expression on her face. "Castaway Party?"

Even Liz laughed and shook her head. "Gloria broke her leg on her honeymoon and they took the cast off a few days before we came on this trip."

"The worst three months of my life," Gloria muttered.

"She grumbled and groaned about her stinkin' cast the entire time!" Lucy explained.

"So we decided to throw her a castaway party to celebrate," Margaret said.

Ruth plucked a permanent marker from her pocket. "We even brought markers so everyone could sign it."

"Where did..." Gloria started to ask.

"Paul gave it to me before we left," Dot said.

"Gather around the table. I'll take a picture," Frances said.

The girls squeezed in at the table and posed for several pictures before Millie switched spots and took a few more.

They all made a big deal of autographing the cast and Liz, the artist, drew a stick person with her leg in a hole and "x's" for eyes.

"Very funny," Gloria grimaced. It was all in good fun and she wasn't angry, just relieved the cast was on the picnic table instead of plastered to her leg.

The girls thoroughly enjoyed their afternoon as they soaked up the sun, swam in the crystal clear water, and snorkeled along the edge of the rocks.

Lunchtime arrived and the girls settled in at the table, anxious to see what delicious goodies Annette and Amit had packed.

"I have no idea what's in here," Millie said. She pulled out several large food containers. The first one contained a variety of pinwheel wraps. Some had turkey, some had ham while others were roast beef. There were even a few with all three meats.

The second plastic storage container was full of creamy bacon potato salad.

Millie's eyes lit when she pulled it out. "Oh! This is the best. Annette has some super-secret potato salad recipe. It has bacon, sharp cheddar cheese and instead of using only mayonnaise, she mixes it with sour cream, too."

"I bet it's delicious," Dot said.

The last container was full of ripe, red watermelon wedges.

Millie placed everything on the table, along with several bottled waters.

The girls prayed over their food, thanking God for rescuing the Siren of the Seas crew and for blessing them with a beautiful day on the island of St. Croix.

When they finished eating there were only a few scraps left.

Millie lifted the lid on the cooler and started to put the empty containers back inside when she realized she had missed one last container. "Uh-oh. I forgot one." She pulled it out, set it on the table and lifted the lid.

Inside the container was a cake shaped like a cast. At the bottom of the cake was a protruding digit that looked like a big toe. The toenail was painted red.

Millie sliced off a large piece, put it on a paper plate and handed it to Gloria. The white sheet cake was filled with vanilla pudding and the cream cheese frosting was a pale shade of pink.

The cake was delicious and Gloria quickly devoured her piece. She popped the last bite of the rich creamy cake in her mouth. "So what happened to the hijackers?" she asked her cousin.

"Whew!" Millie shook her head. "You're never gonna believe this one."

She told the story of how Ingrid Kozlov confessed to helping plan the hijacking. She had told Staff Captain Vitale and Pursuer Donovan Sweeney her main computer monitor was on the fritz and had put in a request for a new system. Majestic Cruise Lines, along with Captain Armati, had approved the expense.

The only problem was there wasn't a problem with the monitor at all. Ingrid had placed her "order" with a fake company, set up by the ringleader of the hijack operation, Boris Smirnov. Smirnov purchased a monitor, disassembled it and removed all of the guts.

He filled the inside of the computer with an array of assault rifles, ammo, small hand grenades and other weapons.

When the computer arrived at the cruise port on Saturday, Ingrid personally signed for it, and even supervised the delivery and "installation."

The other suspects/hijackers arrived, disguised as passengers and once everything was in place, they simultaneously overpowered the engine room crew and bridge staff.

Ingrid didn't want Captain Armati or the others to know she was part of the operation so she anonymously placed an order for a birthday cake for the captain with specific instructions on when it was to be delivered.

The hijackers used the delivery of the cake - and an unsuspecting Amit - to gain access to the bridge.

The first thing they did was scramble communications with the outside world while their co-conspirators aboard the yacht sent a ransom demand to the cruise line. They used the yacht, stationed not far from the cruise ship, as their point of contact to ensure passengers and crew were not able to reach authorities.

"Authorities intercepted a communication a couple days before the ship set sail. It was unclear which cruise ship the hijackers were targeting so they placed sea marshals on all ships leaving the port."

"Which would explain why the crew from the other cruise ship told some of the crew on our ship about the heightened security," Lucy said.

"Exactly," Millie nodded. "According to Ingrid, Boris had already planned the first casualty of their mission. It was to be Dave Patterson, Head of Security."

"What about the small lifeboat that was headed back to San Juan in search of help?" Gloria asked.

"They made it safely to shore and were in the process of getting help when we regained control of the ship. Siren of the Seas plans to make a quick detour on its way back to Miami to pick up both the crew and the lifeboat."

Millie finished her last bite of cake and glanced at her watch. "I better get back. I have to help Andy greet guests as they make their way back onto the ship."

The girls helped her pack everything up, all unanimously deciding they had had enough sun for the day and headed back to the ship.

When they got to the end of the beach, they all glanced behind them at the beautiful private oasis they had just left.

"Today was so much fun," Andrea said.

"It was fun," Millie declared. "Maybe you should make this an annual girls' event and cruise again with us again next year!"

The end.

The series continues. Look for Book #7, coming soon.

If you enjoyed reading "Cruise Control", please take a moment to leave a review.. It would be greatly appreciated! Thank you!

Get Free Books And More

Sign up for my Free Cozy Mysteries Newsletter to get free and discounted books, giveaways & soon-to-be-released books!

hopecallaghan.com/newsletter

Creamy Bacon Potato Salad

<u>Ingredients</u>:

5 lbs. red potatoes, cooked, cooled and cut into wedges (can sub yellow potatoes)
1 cup mayonnaise
2 cups sour cream (regular or light)
4 eggs, cooked, cooled and chopped
10 slices of bacon, fried and crumbled (reserve a couple tbsp. of the grease!)
1 cup sharp or extra sharp cheddar cheese
4 pieces scallion, finely chopped
1 stalk celery finely chopped (optional)
Salt to taste
Pepper to taste

<u>Directions</u>:

Mix mayonnaise, sour cream, chopped eggs, crumbled bacon, cheddar cheese, chopped scallion, celery, and salt and pepper in large bowl. Add 1 – 2 tablespoons of bacon grease. Blend.

Add cooked potatoes and mix well.

Refrigerate after mixing.

Made in United States
Orlando, FL
19 November 2021

10521642R00187